EVER CARING

CAROLYNE AARSEN

Misty Ridge
Publishing

CHAPTER ONE

*J*ust go in. *It's just an office. A building.*

Renee stood just outside the door of Arlan Truscott, Barrister and Solicitor, surprised that the pounding of her heart wasn't echoing in the entrance.

The last time she'd been here, she'd sat in Arlan's office and signed papers that haunted her still.

That was nine long years ago.

With a decisive nod and a quick sucking in of her breath, she pushed the door open and entered the office.

The woman sitting behind the wooden desk dominating the reception area looked up, a headset nested in her teased blond hair, and smiled. "Hey, Renee, you're early."

"I hope that's okay?" Renee asked, her eyes flicking over the interior of the office, noting the changes.

Now the walls were painted a soft, colonial blue instead of the puce-green imprinted on her memory. A color that could still make her nauseous. She clutched the handle of her shoulder bag and suppressed the dark thoughts, turning back to Debbie. "Is Mr. Truscott ready to see me?"

"There's been a change in plans. Mr. Truscott was called away, but his son, Tate, will take over your file."

That was puzzling, but she was secretly relieved. Though Rockyview wasn't large, she still ran into Mr. Truscott from time to time. Though it got easier, once in awhile the memories would assault her but over time she had learned to smooth off the rough edges. However, sheer necessity had forced her to set up an appointment with him today.

"Have you met Tate?" Debbie asked.

"No. Not yet," Renee said. "Though I have heard about him."

Then the door of the other office opened, and Renee got to her feet to meet Tate Truscott herself.

He looked to be in his mid-thirties, tall, slender, thick blond hair waving away from a strong-featured face. His blue eyes flicked from the file he held to her, and when he smiled, she couldn't stop an answering lift of her heart.

Classically handsome, she thought, yet with eyes that seemed to hold a shadow of sadness. Through her friend Evangeline, Renee had heard that Tate Truscott was a widower, that he had a young daughter and that he'd moved to Rockyview from Toronto two weeks ago to help his father with his growing legal business. Evangeline knew all this because Tate boarded his horses at her father's ranch.

"Good morning, Ms. Albertson," Tate said, holding his hand out to take hers. "I'm Tate Truscott. I'm sorry my father couldn't see you this morning. He had some unexpected business to take care of."

Renee took his hand, his firm grip creating the faintest tingle in her palm.

She shook her feelings aside, attributing them as a normal reaction to an attractive male. She was still single, after all, as her mother frequently pointed out to her.

As if she had any time for men. She had a disabled mother to take care of and a business to sell. And it was the latter that brought her here today.

"My father gave me your file this morning," Tate said, standing aside to let her precede him into his office. He walked around the desk and dropped into the chair across from her. "He said you're in the process of selling your business?"

Renee nodded, settling into the straight-backed wooden chair across from him. As she did, she darted a quick glance around the room, stifling the chills that chased each other down her spine as memories intruded. This was a different time. Different lawyer. Different office.

The walls in here were painted a cheerful yellow. A large bookcase covered one wall with the usual assortment of legal books. To one side, however, she saw a small red table and chair covered with papers and crayons and paints. A pink electronic device sat on one corner of the table emitting a glowing green light. On the wall above that table was an assortment of framed pictures. One of them was of a stunningly beautiful woman. She held the hand of a little girl with tousled blond hair and a gap-toothed smile. They were backlit by a large window that over-looked the city of Toronto.

Taken from the CN Tower, Renee assumed, her heart turning over at the sight of the little girl.

"That's my daughter," Tate said, catching the direction of Renee's curious gaze. "Addison. She's eight."

"She's adorable," Renee said past the sudden thickness in her throat. Why did this happen to her every time she saw a girl of that age?

Please, Lord, help me concentrate. Help me let go. That was in the past. I've moved on.

Her prayer eased her heartbeat back to normal, then she looked back at Tate. "How does she like living in Rockyview?" she asked, determined to have an ordinary conversation. "I imagine it's quite a change from Toronto."

"She loves it. Especially because we have a place to keep our horses that's closer than where we boarded them in Ontario."

"So you and your daughter ride?"

"Not as often as we'd like, but I'm hoping that will change once we're settled in. Addison and I are still trying to find a rhythm here, and I'm trying not to worry about her all the time. Hard to break old habits," he said.

She caught an edge of tension in his voice and wondered once again about his situation. Rumor had it that his wife had died almost a year ago. That was why he'd moved back to Rockyview.

"But enough about that." Tate flipped open the manila folder and pulled out a piece of paper, obviously getting back to business.

She couldn't help a niggling regret. Tate seemed easy to talk to, and she had enjoyed the ordinary conversation they had shared, even for a moment. It had been a while since she'd had a normal interaction with a man. Any guy she had dated since her mother's accident had to deal with the reality that Renee's mother and her disabilities were a priority for her. None of them could.

"So you want to sell your business?" Tate was saying, his voice anchoring her back to the present.

Renee nodded. "Yes, the buyer, Cathy, is eager to get the final paperwork done and so am I. I'm assuming that's why your father called me here?"

Tate sat back in his chair. He wore a white button-down shirt with a tie, but the tie was loosened, and the cuffs of the sleeves were rolled up. He looked casually disheveled yet had an air of command, which felt oddly reassuring.

"Unfortunately, we can't sign off on the sale just yet."

Renee felt cold bloom in her chest. "Why not?" Things had to get moving. Her mother's appointments to see the therapist were scheduled. They needed the money from this sale before the treatment began, and she didn't want Ned and Cathy, the buyers, to change their minds. Her kind of business was niche and required someone with a measure of expertise.

"There's been a builder's lien filed against the property about three days ago."

"What? By whom? The renovations on the store were finished two months ago." Fixing up the back rooms of the store had cost her more than she had budgeted for, but it had been a condition of the sale, which had been delayed a couple of times already. "I paid Benny Alpern in full for his work."

"Benny was the general contractor?" Tate asked, glancing down at the file again.

"That's correct," Renee said, trying not to let panic overwhelm her as she leaned forward. She'd had a hard enough time just coming to this office—now things wouldn't be finalized today? And, worse, the sale would be put off? What would happen to her mother? The clock was ticking, and she was running out of time.

Renee drew in a long, slow breath, forcing herself to remain calm.

"The lien was put on by an electrician named Freddy Peckham. He claims the general contractor, Benny Alpern, owed him some money, and Benny claims he doesn't. Neither seems to want to budge."

Renee dropped back in her chair, frustrated. "So I can't sell this property until they figure it out."

"Sorry. Afraid not." He gave her a crooked smile, which didn't help her fragile equilibrium.

"But I have to sell the property soon," she said. "I need the money for my mother's—" She stopped herself there. Tate Truscott was a virtual stranger. He didn't need to know the complicated issues of her life.

She folded her arms, her thoughts chasing each other around

her tired head. There was too much to think about and not enough emotional reserve to deal with it.

She thought of her mother, confined to a wheelchair, and the therapy program they'd heard about that could potentially allow her to walk again.

The therapist was in Vancouver, well over a thousand miles away from Rockyview. The program would take a year, and to pay for it, Renee was selling her store.

But now?

"How much money does Freddy need?" Renee asked, trying to find a solution.

"According to the lien he filed, about ten thousand dollars."

"What?" Renee shot up in her chair. "Is he kidding? I can't believe he did that much work on the store reno."

Tate glanced down at the file again, the light casting his face in shadows. "He's claiming he wasn't reimbursed for work or materials and that's what his battle is with Mr. Alpern."

"Well, he's wrong." Renee shook her head. "I'll have to talk to him about that." She didn't look forward to that. Freddy was a strange duck. She hadn't wanted him doing the renovations on the store, but Benny had said he was good. And cheap.

Obviously not so cheap after all.

She kneaded the bridge of her nose, trying to settle her ragged emotions, wishing time would stop its steady wheeling.

The past few months had been a marathon. Attending doctor's and therapist's appointments for her mother, making the hard decisions to sell a business she had poured her heart and soul into since its humble beginnings.

Now she had Freddy to deal with, plus Ned and Cathy Meckle, the already-skittish future owners of the store, to placate.

"Are you okay, Ms. Albertson? Can I get you something to drink?" Tate's worried voice yanked her out of her fog of anxious thoughts.

She looked up, surprised at the concern on his features. "I'm sorry. Just trying to figure out when I'll have time to talk to Cathy Meckle, the buyer."

"I can deal with Freddy and Benny. As for Mrs. Meckle, don't worry about her. She's calling this afternoon. I can let her know what the problem is," he said, a careful smile lifting one corner of his mouth. "We'll take care of you."

Renee held his steady gaze. The confidence and assurance in his voice eased her concern. "Thanks. That would be helpful," she said, thankful for his thoughtfulness.

He's getting paid to do this, a cynical voice reminded her.

But in spite of that, as she looked into his deep blue eyes, she felt a curious connection. A feeling that she would be, as he said, taken care of. It was a good feeling. One she hadn't experienced in awhile.

Then her cell phone vibrated, and with an apologetic look toward Tate, she pulled it out of her purse and glanced at it.

"Sorry. I have to take this," she said. "It's my mother."

Tate held up his hand. "No problem. We'll be in touch."

She nodded, then touched the screen to answer the call as she exited Tate's office.

"Hey, Mom. Are you okay?" Renee couldn't stop the flicker of concern that always accompanied a phone call from her mother. Her pain had increased of late, and though she would never tell her, Renee knew. Could see it on her mother's pinched mouth and her forced cheerfulness on the mornings when she'd had an especially restless night.

"Everything is all right," her mother assured her. "I just wanted to know how your visit with Tate, I mean, Mr. Truscott, went."

"Oh. Fine," Renee said, waving a distracted hand toward Debbie, who waved back. "We'll talk about it later." She wasn't sure how she would break the news about the possible postponement of the sale.

"Are you coming back to the store?"

"After I get some groceries," she said, navigating the narrow stairs leading down to the street. "Is everything okay? I can come now if you want."

"No. I'm fine. Everything is just fine, honey." Her mother's voice held a cheerful note that, in spite of all the work and decisions piling up in Renee's life the past few months, made the stress of selling the store and moving worthwhile. Ever since they started talking about the therapy program in Vancouver and the possibility that her mother would be able to walk again, she had been smiling more. Seemed happier.

"So I'll see you later?" her mother asked.

"Hopefully in half an hour," Renee said. She said goodbye and ended the call.

But as she stepped out into the street, a curious thought occurred to her.

How did her mother know she was meeting with Tate when she didn't know herself until she got to the office?

※※※※

Relax. Just relax. Rockyview is a small town. Addison is only ten minutes late. She is probably looking at something in a store window.

In spite of his thoughts, however, Tate's fingers trembled as he punched in the numbers of his daughter's cell phone, scanning the streets downtown for any sign of his eight-year-old daughter.

Finally she answered. "Hey, Daddy," she chirped. "I can see you."

Tate stopped, forcing his pounding heart to slow down. This wasn't downtown Toronto. This was Rockyview, population seven thousand. She's okay.

Of course, he didn't know how okay she would be once he

met up with her. She was supposed to have been in his office ten minutes ago.

"I can see you but you can't see me," Addison taunted as he shot his gaze up and down the main street of the town, his eyes grazing over the brick buildings with their crenellated roofs and fancy brickwork looking for his daughter. In the distance he heard the rumble of the train approaching, then the warning wail of its horn. In a few seconds he wouldn't be able to hear Addison over the roar of the train. "Where are you?"

"I'm at Scrap Happy. It's a fun, fun place, Daddy."

Scrap Happy? That was Renee Albertson's store.

He relaxed as the fear and worry that had turned his heart to a block of ice melted away. "So where is that?" he asked.

"Turn around, Dad."

He turned, then saw his daughter waggling her fingers at him from inside a store, standing behind a colorful window display of scrapbooks, cards, umbrellas and seashells, her blond hair catching the light from the display. Then he heard a woman's voice call her and Addison disappeared.

He shoved the door of the store open, the bell above the door tinkling out an erratic welcome.

He knew he was overreacting to her lateness, but ever since his wife, Molly, had been killed by a car only a block from their home, Tate had felt vulnerable and overprotective.

Especially because Addison was supposed to have been with Molly that day.

His eyes adjusted from the bright sunlight outside, and as they did, his gaze slipped past the carousels of stickers, rows of papers and shelves holding bottles of glitter, shiny paint and a rainbow assortment of ribbons and buttons.

Addison, however, was nowhere in sight. Nor was Blythe, her babysitter.

He navigated his way through the shelves of scrapbooking supplies and finally found Addison at the back of the store standing beside an older woman in a wheelchair. The woman looked to be about fifty, her graying hair pulled back in a loose ponytail, and when she turned to them, he caught a faint resemblance to Renee Albertson in her heart-shaped face and the upward tilt of her eyebrows. He guessed this was Renee's mother. His father had mentioned that Mrs. Albertson had been in a car accident that had left her paralyzed.

Addison's grin almost split her face as she ran toward him, her hair streaming behind her. She grabbed his hand and pulled with a strength surprising for an eight-year-old.

"Come and see, Dad. This is the coolest thing," she announced, dragging him toward Mrs. Albertson, who was looking over at him now with an expression of interest.

"Good afternoon, Mr. Truscott," she said with a wide smile. "I'm glad to see you here."

He looked over to Addison, trying to keep his voice light and nonthreatening. "Honey, you're supposed to come to the office right away after school."

Addison's expression shifted. "I'm sorry. I wanted to see the store. Blythe said she would tell you." Her lip quivered and she dropped her head in sorrow.

He felt instantly contrite. It wasn't her fault he had overreacted. "It's okay," he said, trying to reassure her. "I was just worried."

"Children do that to us, don't they," Mrs. Albertson said, looking up at him with a smile. "From the moment they're born, they make us vulnerable and scared."

Tate laughed lightly. "You can say that again." He glanced down at Addison, remembering all too well his feeling of utter helplessness when that tiny baby was placed in his arms.

And behind that a rush of love so full, he knew his life would never be the same.

Addison tugged on his hand again. "Look at these cards," Addison was saying. "Aren't they pretty? Renee teaches people how to make them. She also does printing stuff. What do you think of it?"

Tate obediently glanced at the cards lying on the table beside Mrs. Albertson. "Very pretty," he said, not sure what else he was supposed to say about the colorful stacks of paper and glitter. "Now we should go."

"We could make some cards. Together." Addison looked up at him, and must have sensed his hesitation. "Don't you think that would be fun?"

"That might not be your father's idea of a good time," a gentle but husky voice spoke out behind him.

Tate was surprised at the imperceptible lift Renee's sudden presence created.

He turned to look at her as she came around the display of papers. Yesterday when she came to his office she wore her hair pulled back, a suit jacket, tailored shirt and pencil skirt, which, combined with her somewhat-reserved attitude, had given her an aloof air. She looked all business.

Today she wore a pink shirt, blue jeans and sandals. Her light brown hair was loose, falling around her heart-shaped face.

Today she looked softer, more feminine. More appealing.

He brushed aside his reaction. He was in no place emotionally to allow another person into his and Addison's lives. He pulled his attention back to his daughter.

"Where is Blythe?" Tate asked.

Renee waved a slender hand. "I was showing her some accents she could use on her scrapbook. I'll go find her."

As she spoke, Blythe appeared from behind the rack of paper, staring down at a package, as if reading the contents. Her dark hair stuck up in gelled spikes glistening in the overhead lights of the store, at odds with the plaid schoolgirl skirt and slouchy sweater she wore today. "Hey, sweetie, there you are," she said, glancing over at Addison. "We should go. Don't want your dad to..."

Her voice trailed off as she caught sight of Tate. "Hey, Mr. Truscott," she said with an airy wave. "Did you get my message?"

Tate was momentarily taken aback. "What message?"

"That Addison and I would be late today." Blythe gave him a tentative smile. "I called your cell phone and left a message. Every time we walk by this store, Addison wants to stop in, and today I said it was okay as long as it was okay with you. And then you didn't call back and we were coming past and Addison was pulling at my hand—"

"It's okay," he said, stopping her midgush. "Everything is fine."

It wasn't really, but he wasn't getting into a discussion about Blythe's responsibilities in front of strangers or the fact that he didn't think to check his messages before imagining his daughter either lying injured on the street or in the hospital. He turned back to Addison, who was leaning against Mrs. Albertson's wheelchair. The sight of the little girl and the older woman caught at his heart. His own mother had died when he was young, and Molly's mother and father lived overseas. Addison didn't have a grandmother in her life.

"We should go, honey. I need to get back to work," Tate told his daughter. "And I'm sure Renee and Mrs. Albertson have their own things to do."

"Okay. I'll go." Addison cast a wistful glance around the colorful store as if comparing it to her father's dull office, then heaved a long-suffering sigh and trudged past Blythe out the store.

Tate hesitated a moment, and without knowing why, looked back at Renee and her mom, Brenda.

Renee was watching Addison, her arms crossed over her chest, a curious mixture of fear and sorrow on her face. Then she turned her head, and as their eyes met, he felt it again. A connection. An awareness.

Then she turned and the moment faded away.

You're a widower with a daughter who is still grieving, he reminded himself. *You don't need the mess of another relationship.*

And definitely not someone like Renee, who, it seemed, had her own priorities.

CHAPTER TWO

"Sure, Tate Truscott is good-looking—I won't argue that." Renee took another sip of her coffee and sat back in the soft leather chair tucked in a back room of Shelf Awareness, Evangeline's bookstore. "But I'm not interested."

She looked around the room, allowing the ambience of the store to wash away the stress of the day. She had tried to contact Benny and Freddy but it seemed neither wanted to talk to her. She'd had to keep her frustration stifled because her mother, with her radar senses, would guess something was wrong and then she'd stress.

But for now she tried to relax at the room in the shop dedicated to book club.

The walls were lined with shelves filled with Evangeline's personal library. Evangeline lived above the shop in a small apartment that couldn't begin to hold all the books she owned so she had put many down here.

Leather recliners, worn-fabric occasional chairs and a long, low-slung couch were scattered through the room, creating a welcoming and eclectic atmosphere. Bright paintings, done by local schoolchildren, hung on the one wall that wasn't taken up with shelves.

Twice a month on Tuesdays, Evangeline, Mia Verbeek, Renee, Amy and a variety of other women met in this room to discuss a book chosen by one of the members. The discussion was often lively, as the main members of the book club had varying tastes in books.

"Why wouldn't you be interested in Tate Truscott?" Evangeline asked, lowering herself into the armchair across from Renee, her long skirt draping artfully over her legs. She swept her wavy brown hair back from her face and secured it with an elastic, enhancing her delicate features. "He's handsome, eligible and elegant. I'm trying to imagine him in a cutaway and cravat. Absolutely perfect." Evangeline sighed dramatically, obviously very taken with Mr. Truscott herself.

"I think it's time you return to the real world and get your nose out of your Regency novels," Renee said with a faint snort, wishing her friend would get off the topic of Tate Truscott. "As for eligibility, he's a recent widower, and he has a little girl. I'm sure he's not looking to date. And I've got my mother and all the responsibilities that come with her."

Evangeline frowned at that and Renee felt immediately guilty.

"I don't mean to say that I resent them."

"I know you don't," Evangeline said. "No one would ever think that. But wouldn't it be nice to indulge in a little romance?"

"There's no such thing as a little romance," Renee said, smiling at her friend despite her own feelings on the matter. "Not between someone who had a daughter and someone who is moving away as soon as she can sell her store."

"I know, but he's so good looking."

Renee tried to ignore her friend by paging through a book lying on the table beside her.

Tate had been taking up too much space in her mind as it was. He and his little girl. She was surprised at the pain she felt when she saw the little girl. Addison was too glaring a reminder of what she had given up all those years ago.

"Doesn't he even appeal a little?"

Renee wished Evangeline would stop. She had her own struggles with love and romance. "Even if he does, like I said, I live in the real world."

"The real world? Like what's in those depressing highbrow novels you read?" Evangeline kicked off her sandals and tucked her feet under her skirt. "I'll stick with my happy-ever-afters, thank you very much."

"But my books generate the best discussions," Renee returned, just as the door behind them opened again.

Renee saw Mia enter through the store's back entrance.

"That's because everyone wants to talk about how much they hated them," Mia said as she set her book bag down on the small table in the middle of the room and hung her jacket up on the hooks just inside the door. She shoved her hands through her short-cropped black hair and blew out a sigh. She poured herself a cup of coffee from the carafe on the table behind Renee and dropped onto the empty couch across from Renee and Evangeline. Taking a sip of coffee, she leaned back and closed her eyes. "Ah. Bliss. I've been clinging to the promise of this moment for the past ten hours."

"Busy day in the flower shop?" Renee asked, feeling sympathy for her friend. Mia was a single mother of four children and ran the flower shop full-time. Renee, who only had her mother to take care of, couldn't imagine how Mia managed.

"The flower shop is the easiest part of my life," Mia said, nudging her running shoes off her feet and wiggling her toes. "It's the boys who are wearing me down, not the twins. Thank goodness Blythe came early today to help me out. She got another babysitting job so I hope she doesn't bail on me. I need that girl in my life." She sighed, rolled her shoulders and looked around. "No one else coming tonight?"

"I don't know about April, Amy or Emily, but Jennie is coming. Though she said she didn't care for the book we had to read," Evangeline said, casting an arch look Renee's way.

"Told you," Mia said with a curt nod. "Depressing."

Renee was about to challenge her opinion, when Evangeline spoke up. "Renee finally met Tate Truscott."

Mia lifted one eyebrow and nodded. "What did you think?"

"Why is everyone making a fuss about this guy?" Renee tried not to sound peeved.

"Single. Good-looking. What's not to fuss about," Evangeline said with a gleam in her eye.

"I'm not in the market," Renee retorted.

"You haven't been in the market since Ted," Evangeline said.

"Ted didn't count." Mia waved Renee's previous boyfriend off with a flick of her hand, as if getting rid of a pesky fly. "Nor did Kent or Scott. None of them lasted longer than four months."

That was because none of them could handle the reality that Renee's mother was part of the deal. And once Renee had found out about the new therapy plan available for her mother in Vancouver, she hadn't bothered getting involved with anyone else. Why get involved with anyone when she was leaving as soon as she could.

"Dwight was your last serious boyfriend," Evangeline murmured. "And that was over nine years ago."

"Are we still talking about him?" Renee shot Evangeline a warning look. "That guy is more historical than your books."

"Sorry," Evangeline said. "I just thought of him because I saw his mother in town yesterday. She told me he was married and living in Australia. I didn't think he'd ever settle down."

"Neither did I," Renee said.

Renee had buried that part of her past long ago. She and

Dwight had dated all through high school, much to her parents' chagrin. Dwight was bad news and she knew it. But he was popular and was invited to all the best parties. When her father died, at the beginning of their first year of college, Renee's mother was lost in her own grief, and Renee drowned herself in a lifestyle full of drinking and partying. And Dwight.

The consequences of those mistakes were still affecting her and her mother's life. She preferred to keep Dwight and any memories of him buried deep.

"You were well rid of him when he decided to hightail it out of here," Mia said.

"Trust me, I'm not pining for Dwight—or any man," Renee said. "I've got enough going on in my life right now."

"You're probably right to avoid Tate anyway," Mia said, taking a sip of her coffee. "I heard that Kerry at Mug Shots tried to set him up with someone, but he told her flat out he wasn't interested, and then he turned down a date with Tiffany Newton."

"I'm sure Renee could make him change his mind," Evangeline said. "You're way better looking than Tiffany."

"So what did you all think of the book?" Renee asked, bringing the subject back to the book club and away from romantic entanglements.

"I think I'd like to talk about why I saw Tate Truscott come to your store today," Evangeline said, shooting Renee an arch glance over the top of her coffee mug. "I don't think he was there to make cards or a scrapbook. Though he could have been there to order some brochures for the office. Hmmm..."

"He came to pick up his daughter," Renee retorted, cutting off Evangeline's romantic wanderings. "She stopped by the store with Blythe. And that's the only reason he came."

When the words left her mouth, she regretted it. She should have simply smiled, nodded and moved on.

Evangeline gave her a cheeky grin and looked as if she was

about to say more, but thankfully was interrupted when the door opened again.

Jennie Bond entered with Sophie Brouwer, the two chattering away like the good friends they were.

Jennie lowered herself into a chair beside Renee and heaved out a sigh. "Busy day today," she said as if to explain why she was late.

"Were you helping in school again?" Renee asked as Jennie pulled out her book from the bag she had taken along.

"The teacher asked me to read with a little girl who just moved here," Jennie replied, adjusting her glasses. Though Jennie was past retirement age, she occasionally helped at the school. Her granddaughter, Hailey, was a teacher there and often asked her to come. "Her name is Addison Truscott. Poor thing's still grieving the death of her mother."

Renee wished her heart didn't beat so hard at the mention of Addison. The little girl created a storm of feelings she didn't know how to navigate. Longing, pain and sorrow. Each created a tug that drew her to the girl one moment and made her want to push her away in another.

"Everything okay?" Mia asked, laying her hand on Renee's arm. "You look upset."

Renee jerked her attention back to her friend and waved off her concern. "No, I'm sorry. Just got lots on my mind."

"I imagine you do," Mia said. "What with trying to sell the store and your mother's treatment plan. Lots to deal with."

Renee nodded. "More than enough. I don't have any room for anything else in my life," she said with a warning tone. She didn't want to talk about Tate, and she especially didn't want to talk about his daughter. Thankfully, she wouldn't be seeing too much of them anytime soon.

"Can I ask you a question, Daddy?"

Tate finished up the sentence he was typing out then glanced at Addison, sitting in one corner of his office, drawing. "Sure, honey, what is it?"

Addison sat, elbows planted on her table, swinging her feet. Crayons and papers lay strewn about her, imitating the mess spread out over his desk. "My one friend isn't being very nice to me and I was trying so hard to be nice to her."

"Which friend is this?" Tate made himself turn away from the computer to give his daughter his full attention, trying not to let his work pull at him. While Blythe was able to pick Addison up from school she wasn't able to watch her every day. So Addison would come and sit in the office and watch shows on her iPad or draw and color.

"Talia. She's usually lots of fun and she said she's my best friend. But yesterday I wanted her to work with me on my Math Facts but she went to work with Natasha instead. I don't think I like her anymore."

Tate fought down an immediate reprimand. Addison needed a listening ear right now.

"Did you try to ask her why she didn't want to work with you?"

"I wanted to but Talia said she had to help Natasha." Addison frowned at him, as if he was being deliberately obtuse. "I think she's being mean to me. I think she doesn't want to be my friend anymore."

Tate wasn't sure what to say or how to navigate this territory. Truth to tell, he had been so busy building his law practice that the bulk of Addison's upbringing had been taken care of by his wife.

Maybe that's why she was unfaithful?

Tate fought down the accusing voice. He always tried to be home by suppertime, making sure he was around to put Addison to bed.

"Honey, sometimes there are things going on in people's lives that we don't know about," he said, trying to find a diplomatic way to let her know he cared but also not to take things so personally. "Maybe she's not being mean to you, maybe the teacher asked her to help Talia."

Addison seemed to consider this then shrugged. "Maybe," she said, then pushed her crayons aside. "And right now, I'm bored. I don't like being in the office so long."

"I know, honey. Give me another hour and then we can go."

"Another hour?" she whined.

Tate glanced at the file, then at the clock. His father was always reminding him that right now Addison should be his priority. But Tate still wanted to pull his share of the workload. He had just come here and wanted to prove himself, so to speak. "Okay, maybe half an hour, then we can leave for the ranch."

"I don't want to go to the ranch."

"You haven't seen the horses since we dropped them off last week," he said. "What else would you want to do?"

"I don't know." She sighed again, and Tate shot her a concerned look. Ever since Molly died Addison had been drifting along, a lifeless little shell of a girl, not excited or enthusiastic about anything.

He thought moving to Rockyview to be close to his father as well as having the horses closer would help lift her out of her funk. And it had, for a while, but she'd drifted back into the same lethargy that had gripped her since he and Addison had walked away from Molly's grave.

In fact, the only time he'd seen Addison excited about anything was yesterday at Renee Albertson's store.

"Do you want to go out for dinner tonight?" he pressed. "We could go to the Dairy Queen. Peanut-buster parfaits?"

"I miss my mommy," she said, her voice wobbling.

Sorrow gathered in his chest at his daughter's plaintive words. Ever since Molly's death, his entire focus had been the well-being of his precious daughter. He had stayed in Toronto so she could finish school. Had put off moving here so she could work through her grief.

She was the reason he'd given up his huge salary at a prestigious firm and moved here to join his father's law firm once he thought enough time had elapsed. He wanted to give Addison the family she never had during his and Molly's shaky marriage.

He had always been careful not to say anything negative about Molly, but at times Addison's grief over her mother disturbed him. Molly hadn't deserved such sorrow.

"Of course you do," he murmured, his heart melting at the sight of the tear tracking down his daughter's cheek. "Come here, honey," he said, pushing himself away from his desk and holding out his hands.

She shuffled toward him and climbed onto his lap. He cuddled her close, barely able to get her head under his chin. When did she get so big?

"Someday you won't fit on my lap anymore," he murmured, stroking her head with his chin.

"I'll always sit on your lap because I'll always be your little girl," she announced. "But someday I won't be your only girl."

"What do you mean?"

"Grandpa was saying he hoped you would get married again. If you do, I won't be your only girl anymore."

A chill washed over him. "When did Grandpa say that?"

"Last night. He was talking to Aunt Sally on the phone."

Aunt Sally was his mother's sister and lived back in their old hometown of Radium. Though his mother had died when Tate was young, his father had stayed in close contact with her, even after his father moved here to Rockyview. And Aunt Sally was never short on advice.

"I don't think you need to worry about me getting married again," Tate promised his daughter.

"Why won't you?"

Too complicated, Tate wanted to say. Marrying Molly had caused him a world of hurt. He'd truly thought she was the one for him when they met. Even after enduring three miscarriages, they'd been happy, and when they finally adopted Addison, Tate truly thought his and Molly's life was complete.

His perfect life started unraveling, however, when Addison was a year old. Tate had discovered that Molly had been unfaithful to him. She'd promised to change. They moved to Toronto for a fresh start, and for a while life seemed good. Until he found out that she'd cheated again.

Though it seemed harsh to think, her death a year ago was a mercy. At least Addison was spared the nastiness of a prolonged divorce and custody battle.

"Grandpa and Aunt Sally think you should get married again."

Tate winced at the thought. He'd been so wrong about Molly. He certainly didn't trust himself to make those promises again to any woman. Nor did he ever want to put himself in a position to be hurt again.

Besides, more than that all, he had Addison to think of. She was his first priority and there was no way he was putting her through any extra stress.

But even as he told himself that, a picture of Renee drifted into his mind, and once again he filed it away under *What Are You Thinking?* Sure she was attractive, but he'd seen attractive women before. So he just had to stay focused.

Tucking his finger under Addison's chin, he tilted her face up. "Grandpa and Aunt Sally shouldn't make decisions for you or me. Right now you're the most important person to me."

Addison gave him a tremulous smile. "God is important, too," she reminded him.

Tate released a semi-embarrassed laugh. "Yes. And God."

His faith had taken a backseat to his personal and professional life the past few years, but coming to Rockyview felt like a renewing of his values. After his father moved here, Tate had visited a couple of times, and he'd appreciated the laid-back ambience of the town. So when it had been time to make a change in his life, this was the first place he'd thought of.

Tate gave Addison a quick kiss, then glanced back at his files. "Let me finish up here, then we'll go to the ranch."

Addison rested her hands on Tate's shoulders, and her expression grew serious. "I want to go to the store again."

"Sure, we can go shopping."

Addison shook her head. "No. I want to go to the scrapbook and printing store." She sat up, looking suddenly animated, grabbing his cheeks between her hands, still sticky from the candy he'd given her. "I saw some really cool books there. With pictures and stuff. We could go there and make a book. We could get stickers and paper and...and all kinds of things and Renee can help me make a book."

Tate frowned, trying to keep up with his daughter's unexpected bubbling enthusiasm. "A book?"

"Of pictures. Of Mommy."

Tate saw his little girl's eyes sparkling with an anticipation he hadn't seen in months. "Do you think you would enjoy making a scrapbook of pictures of Mommy?"

Addison nodded. "I don't like having my pictures of her just in a box. If we put them in a book, then I can look at them better." She jumped off his lap, clapping her hands in anticipation. "That could be so fun. And you could help me. We could do it together."

Tate glanced at his work, then back at his daughter, who was smiling eagerly. Despite his own feelings for Molly and what had happened between them, to Addison, Molly was her mother. And the grief she'd fallen in to was normal. However, maybe making a scrapbook might help her deal with her emotions. Might help her move on.

"Can you wait an hour or so?"

Addison frowned, blinking away the shine of tears. "Can't we do it now? Before the store goes closed?"

Tate blew out a careful sigh as he looked at his daughter, assessing her mood. He knew there were times Addison liked to turn on the tears to manipulate him. And many times they were real. It was an ongoing struggle to sort the two out.

However, this time he figured he may as well err on the side of believing her sorrow to be real.

So he shut off his computer, reminding himself that his father had repeatedly told him to ease back into work, one file at a time.

He'd moved here to make Addison his priority. This could be a way to do it.

And it wouldn't hurt to see Renee again.

Tate was surprised at how thoughts of Renee kept entering his mind. Since Molly's death, he'd never had a problem keeping himself aloof from the flirtatious looks he'd get from some of the single mothers at Addison's dance class or music lessons. None of them appealed to him in any way.

Renee was the first woman who caught his attention and intrigued him on a level he couldn't truly analyze. Strange as it was, he felt as if he knew her.

As they stepped outside, Tate glanced up at the mountains surrounding the town, cradling the valley created by Rockyview and allowed himself a moment to enjoy the view. He felt a sense of peace and well-being he'd never really felt in Toronto.

A young couple passed them while walking their dog. They smiled in greeting, and Addison took a moment to pet the dog, asking a few questions about him.

This was a good place to raise a child, he thought, thankful that he had listened to his father. Maybe, once they settled down, found a place, he could get a dog for Addison. Make a home.

Once they reached the store, Addison ran ahead, pushing the

door open, her enthusiasm easing away any second thoughts Tate had about doing this.

"Hello," she called out. "I'm back."

No one responded, and Addison walked farther inside, but Tate stayed back, feeling out of place amongst the rows of papers and stickers and ribbons.

A movement near the back of the store caught Tate's attention, then he saw Renee step out from behind a row of shelving, carrying a stack of paper.

She wore her hair tied up in a loose ponytail tucked to one side, enhancing her heart-shaped face. Her blue jeans and white shirt gave her a country-girl look that was curiously appealing.

Renee looked up at Tate, her mouth curving in a wistful smile that quickened his heart. Again, he was surprised at his reaction to her.

Then, as Addison came toward her, Renee stumbled to a full stop. Her mouth formed an O of surprise immediately followed by a look of dismay.

And the papers she held slipped out of her arms.

"Here, let me help you with that," Addison said, crouching down to help gather them up.

"It's okay. I got it." Renee's voice held a surprisingly sharp tone as she snatched up the fallen papers.

"I'm really sorry," Addison was saying, obviously noting the reprimand in Renee's voice, as well.

Tate hurried over to help, his defenses coming to the fore. Why was she so upset? It wasn't Addison's fault.

"I'm sure it's fine," he said quietly, his voice holding a faint warning note as he helped. "She didn't mean to startle you."

"No. I know she didn't," Renee said, looking suddenly contrite. "I was just..." She tapped the stack together with trembling hands and slowly rose to her feet. "Sorry, honey. I didn't mean to snap at you. Things have been busy and stressful here... Anyway, I'm sorry."

"No. I'm sorry. I shouldn't have scared you like that," Addison said, clearly eager to make amends.

"What can I help you with?" Renee asked, quickly turning her attention back to Tate.

"Addison wants to make a scrapbook with pictures of her mother." Tate rested a protective hand on his daughter's shoulder. "I understand this is the place to do that."

"Of course," Renee said. "I'm sure we could help you buy what you need."

"But my daddy doesn't know anything about making scrapbooks," Addison said, appealing to Renee. "I want you to help me make it."

"Are you sure you don't want me to help?" Tate asked Addison. "I'm thinking Ms. Albertson is too busy for this."

Especially given her reaction to his daughter. He wanted to protect Addison, not put her in a more difficult spot.

"I want to do it here. This is such a fun store to work in." Addison's voice took on the hurt tone that he knew she did on purpose, but, at the same time, he also knew was often genuine. Besides, he knew working in his office or at his dad's house, where they were staying for now, could not compete with the bright and happy tone of this store.

Tate sensed he wasn't going to change his daughter's mind so he turned back to Renee.

"I would gladly pay for your time," he said, noting that Addison hadn't been this eager about anything in so long, so he was also willing to do whatever it took to make her happy.

"I could come after school with Blythe," Addison chimed in, her voice eager in the face of Renee's obvious reluctance. "So you won't be babysitting me."

Again that moment of hesitation. He sensed this wasn't going to work.

"If it's too much trouble, I'm sure we can figure something else out," Tate added, his voice firm, giving Renee an out. "Who knows, maybe I could learn to make scrapbooks," he said, forcing a grin for his daughter's sake.

"But I want to do it here," Addison said, shooting her father a panicked glance. "In the store. And I want you to help me, Daddy."

"We would gladly help Addison put a scrapbook together," Renee's mother said, rolling her wheelchair toward them. "No need to go somewhere else."

"I'm not sure we'll have the time," Renee sputtered, her gaze flicking from Addison to her mother. "You know we're trying to sell the store."

The sale was on hold until he released the lien, Tate knew. Selling the store wasn't making them busy, so what was the real reason Renee seemed to be putting him and Addison off?

"Of course we'll have the time," Brenda said, her voice holding a note of reprimand.

"But if it's too much trouble..." Addison began, obviously sensing the discord between Renee and her mother.

Renee put her hand to her lips. Then, just as Tate was regretting this spontaneous decision, she looked down at Addison and gave her a tentative smile.

Then she crouched down to make eye contact with her.

"It's not too much trouble. We can help you." Her hand fluttered toward Addison, but then withdrew, as if Renee couldn't make up her mind what to do around his daughter. For a moment Tate caught a fleeting glimpse of pain and sorrow in her eyes that called to him. But as quickly as it appeared, it was gone, making him wonder if he had only imagined it. "Why don't you come tomorrow, and we can start then. We were just closing up the store for the evening."

Addison looked up at her father as if for permission. "Can I come after school and can you come, too?"

For some reason, his daughter was fixated on the idea of

having Renee help her, and Renee seemed as reluctant as her daughter was eager.

His misgivings arose again.

He would have to come with Addison. Create a buffer between her and the reluctant Miss Albertson. Just as he frequently had to do with Molly.

"Sure, sweetie," he said. "We can come tomorrow to start working on the scrapbook."

"Can we come here on Saturday, too?" she asked. "Before we see the horses?"

Though he would have preferred to spend the entire day with Addison, he just nodded. He sensed Addison wasn't going to let go of this until it was done.

"We have horses," Addison explained to Renee. "We keep them at Miss Arsenault's place."

"That's pretty neat," Renee said. "Do you ride?"

Addison nodded enthusiastically. "My mommy took me all the time." Addison's voice broke, and Tate saw Renee's smile waver, as well.

"So I guess Addison will see you tomorrow," he said, filling in the awkward silence. "How long will it take to make the scrapbook?"

Renee shrugged. "It depends on how many pictures you want to include, and how fancy you want it to look."

Tate thought of the large shoebox sitting in Addison's room and shrugged. "I'd like to keep it simple. I can only spend so much time on this project."

Renee bit her lip, shuffling the papers she still held. "Speaking of time, I don't suppose you've heard anything new on how long it will be before the lien is removed?"

Tate shook his head. "I can't get hold of Freddy, and Benny still insists he paid Freddy in full."

"And we can't do anything about that?"

"Not until I contact Freddy or until the lien expires."

"Which is?"

"Freddy has ninety days to prove his case."

"Ninety days? That's too long," she said, panicking. "We have to be in Vancouver in six weeks, and I don't know if Cathy will wait three months to purchase—" She pressed her fingertips to her forehead as if holding herself back from saying anything else. "Should I contact Freddy directly?" she asked. "Light a fire under him? I need this resolved soon."

Tate felt pity for her predicament. His father had told him that Renee wanted to sell the store to pay for an experimental therapy that would, hopefully, help her mother to walk again. He couldn't help but admire her sacrifice.

"No. Don't worry about this. I'll take care of it," Tate said. "It will all work out."

She nodded and gave him a careful smile that, in spite of all that had gone before, still created a flicker of attraction. "I guess we'll just have to wait and see how it goes."

He held her gaze, suddenly unable to look away, and he saw a softening in her expression that quickened his heart.

You can't get involved, he reminded himself. *She's leaving, and you've had enough difficult relationships in your life. You don't need any more.*

CHAPTER THREE

$\mathcal{T}$he chirping of his cell phone broke into Tate's contemplation of the will he had been working on. He glanced at the picture that showed up on the home screen of the phone. Addison.

"Hey, Daddy, where are you?" Addison asked in a singsong voice that he hadn't heard for months. "You're supposed to come to the store, remember?"

"I thought I wasn't supposed to meet you until four o'clock?"

"School closed early. So, can you come?"

"I suppose I can come now," he said, shooting a glance at his desk and the files piled on it. Maybe he could go for a few moments then come back.

"Don't forget the pictures."

"I won't." He disconnected the call, then grabbed the box sitting on Addison's table. She had brought them there this morning before Blythe picked her up to take her to school. Then he stepped out of the office to tell Debbie where he was going just as his father came out of his own office carrying a mug.

"Where's Debbie?" Tate asked.

"Went to the post office. You heading out to see a client?" his father asked, walking over to the coffee machine that Debbie kept going for his father and clients.

"Actually, I'm going to Renee Albertson's store," Tate said, suddenly feeling like a kid caught sneaking out of class early. "I said I'd help Addison with the scrapbook she's doing. I'm going today to see how it all goes." He felt torn. He wanted to be with his daughter in Renee's presence but at the same time he felt like he was ducking out on his responsibilities.

His father nodded, his eyes bright with pleasure. "That's an excellent idea. Addison needs something to keep her mind off her sorrow. This is the perfect solution."

Tate was surprised at his father's enthusiasm. "I'll take work home tonight to get it done. I know it seems silly to take time off to work on some scrapbook..." He let the sentence hang, trying not to feel as if he was letting his father down.

Arlan waved off his objections. "I've told you several times that your main focus should be getting Addison settled in. If helping her with this book at Renee's store helps her get through all of this, then I encourage you to go."

Tate felt a weight slip off his shoulders at his father's understanding words. Back in Toronto, his work had taken precedence over everything: family life, personal life, faith life. There was no way any boss of his would have allowed him to leave work early. Especially to do something as frivolous as work on a scrapbook.

"You better go," his dad said, pushing himself away from the table. "Don't want to keep Re—I mean, Addison, waiting."

Tate shot his father a grin, then headed out the door and down the stairs.

When he stepped into Scrap Happy, he took a moment to get his bearings. An older woman with white, tightly curled hair, wearing a bright pink velour jogging suit, was contemplating a wall filled with shiny plastic packages. A young mother was pushing a buggy with a sleeping baby back and forth, putting sheets of patterned paper into a basket balanced on the hood of the baby's buggy.

Then he heard Renee Albertson's melodic voice, and he followed it to a room in the back.

Addison sat at a table, her tongue clamped between her lips as she cut something out of a piece of pink paper. She glanced up as Tate came in, dropped her scissors and ran to his side.

"Daddy, you finally came," she exclaimed, the unadulterated joy in her voice making him smile.

Then Renee looked up from the table, and as their eyes met, attraction arced between them.

"Look, Renee, my daddy brought the pictures."

When Renee broke the connection and turned toward his daughter, Tate mentally shook his head to get his mind back to the present.

"That's great. Now we can figure out what to do." Renee gave Addison a warm smile, and the concerns he'd felt about Addison working with Renee eased.

"So, how do we start?" Tate asked, pulling up a chair to the table.

Addison was fairly humming with excitement as she pulled open the box.

"The first thing to do is figure out what size album, but Addison already picked one out while we were waiting." Renee sat down across from Addison and showed Tate a small book in Addison's favorite color, purple. "She also told me she wanted to put the pictures in chronological order, and we picked out some of the papers she wants to use."

"You decided all that already?" Tate asked, surprised that Renee seemed so willing to talk to his daughter when she'd been so reticent around her yesterday. "You and Addison?"

Renee nodded, her head bent as if she understood exactly what he was implying.

"I know we didn't get off to the best start," Renee said quietly, sorting through the brightly patterned papers in front of Addison. "But I think things will work out well."

She looked directly at him, and he held her candid gaze, then nodded. He immediately felt bad for his brusque question. Renee was trying, and he was being an overprotective father.

"Thanks for that," he said. "I had a few concerns."

"I understand. I would have, too, given...given my reaction."

He felt the tension in his neck ease at her oblique confession. She was trying, and though he didn't understand what it was about Addison that made her feel so uptight, he had to accept her apology.

He smiled and was pleased to see her smile in return.

She really was pretty, he thought, suddenly unable to look away.

"This was me as a baby," Addison said suddenly, holding out a picture of Molly cuddling her. "I was kind of funny-looking." She dropped that picture on the table and grabbed another one. "Here's my first day of school." She tossed that one aside, too, and grabbed another one as the picture fell to the floor. "This was when I went to dance class and Mommy got sick. Oh, and here's one of my daddy when—"

Tate was about to tell Addison to be careful, when Renee gently laid her hand on Addison's. "Why don't we start at the beginning and sort the pictures out first. You can tell me about them as we go."

Addison frowned at Renee's hand, but when she looked up at Renee, she nodded.

"We want to be careful with the pictures, don't we?" Renee said. "So why don't you pick up the picture you dropped."

"That's okay. I can get it another time." Addison waved off Renee's suggestion.

Then, just as Tate was about to reprimand her, Renee put her hand on Addison's shoulder. "It's just right here," she said, turning her to look at the pictures that had fallen.

Tate's protective instincts rose up at the hurt look he saw on Addison's face from Renee's reprimand. "She just wanted to show you the pictures," he said quietly.

Renee cut him a quick glance, then held up a hand. "Sorry. I wasn't trying to take over your job."

As soon as she spoke, Tate realized how he had sounded. "No. I'm sorry," he said, slanting her a quick smile. "Just being a father."

"That's not a bad thing to be," she returned, adding her own smile.

Their gazes held for a heartbeat longer than they should have, then Renee broke the connection first as she bent down to pick up one of the pictures Addison had tossed on the floor.

She laid the picture down on a piece of white paper. "This would be a good one for the first page. You and your mom and dad leaving the hospital. Do you also have one of you and your mommy or daddy inside the hospital? After you were born? We could put that one with this picture."

Addison leaned over the photo, shaking her head. "I was adopted, so we don't have lots of hospital pictures."

Renee picked up another photo, her fingers trembling, her face suddenly pale. "Where was this one taken?" she choked out as she held up the photo of Molly, Tate and Addison standing in front of the hospital.

Tate smiled at the picture as he took it from her. Sunshine had poured down from the sky that day, and Molly had been happier than she'd been in years. It'd been the most life-changing day of his life.

"It was taken here," he said, gently tracing the bundled figure in Molly's arms. "In Rockyview."

He looked up at Renee, who had her hand on her chest, her face as white as the paper she had been holding seconds before.

"Where were you living at the time?" Her question came out in the faintest of whispers, her face twisted in an expression of near terror.

"I was working as a lawyer. In Whitehorse, in the Yukon Territory."

Renee glanced from the picture to Tate, to Addison, then turned and suddenly ran from the room.

❧

RENEE STOOD in the back alley behind her store, her heart drumming in her chest as what Tate had just told her whirled through her mind.

The picture of Tate and his wife holding a newborn baby was taken in front of Rockyview Hospital.

The baby was Addison.

And Addison was eight.

Reality hit her with the weight of a truck.

Eight years ago Renee had been pregnant. Eight years ago she'd given birth to a baby girl in Rockyview Hospital.

When her boyfriend, Dwight, had found out she was pregnant, he'd broken up with her, leaving her alone to face her mother's disappointment.

The only people who'd stood by Renee were her friends Evangeline and Mia.

Afraid and alone, though her mother had told her repeatedly that she would support her, Renee hadn't seen her way clear to being a single mother.

So she'd visited Mr. Truscott, Tate's father, and told him that she wanted him to facilitate a closed adoption. She didn't want to go through Social Services. Didn't want her mother to find out from any of the people she knew who worked there.

Renee thought she had covered her tracks. Thought she had done everything necessary to put her past behind her.

36

Now the baby she thought had been adopted by a couple living thousands of miles away in the Yukon, the baby she never thought she would ever see again, was sitting in her store. She was real. Sweet. Adorable.

Renee couldn't breathe. Her lungs couldn't pull in enough air.

She pressed her hand against her chest, trying to slow her heart down, wishing time would stop.

Dear Lord, how could this have happened? How could her past have invaded her present so dramatically? Her daughter was supposed to remain safely in the past.

Not here in her present. Not so vividly alive and...here.

She closed her eyes, trying to pull in another breath. Trying to figure out how she was going to process this information.

Her throat closed as the ever-present sorrow raised its dark head. How was she supposed to keep working with Addison now, knowing who she was?

"Renee? What's wrong?" Tate stood in the doorway, concern etched on his features. "Are you okay?"

Reality washed over Renee.

Tate was her little girl's father.

She looked at him as her thoughts tumbled around in her head. "I'm sorry," she mumbled. "I just... The pictures..."

She took another breath, the puzzlement on Tate's face showing her how confused she sounded. But how to explain?

She struggled to gather her thoughts, pull herself back together. He had to know.

She was about to speak, when Addison appeared behind him, peeking around her father, a frown pulling her delicate eyebrows together.

"Are you okay?"

Renee couldn't stop her mind flashing back to the memory of the first time she saw Addison.

A tiny baby, red face, eyes scrunched closed, hair dark as ink.

Too easily Renee remembered how she'd traced her daughter's features and marveled at her delicate eyebrows. Let her miniature fingers curl around hers, the hours and hours of unrelenting labor pain washed away in that precious moment.

She wasn't going to do it, Renee remembered thinking. She was going to keep the baby in spite of her mother lying in a coma in a hospital two hours away. In spite of how impossible it would be for her to raise this baby and take care of her mother on her own.

But then the doctor came to give her an update on her mother just as she was struggling with her decision, this precious child in her arms.

The doctor looked so solemn and Renee felt everything she had imagined, even if only for a few fleeting moments, slipping away.

Her mother's back was broken. There was no way to repair it. Her mother was going to be in a wheelchair for the rest of her life.

Renee knew she couldn't take care of her mother and a baby at the same time. And she knew her first priority was her mother. Given what had happened.

So when the nurse came to take her baby away she relinquished her with a prayer that she would be taken in by a loving family who could give her everything Renee knew she couldn't.

Renee drew in a long, steadying breath as regret and sorrow shivered like icy fingers down her back.

You couldn't take care of her, Renee reminded herself.

Though her mother had promised to help take care of the baby, that promise was untenable when the doctor brought her news of her mother's diagnosis.

She dragged her gaze away from Addison, looking straight ahead at the range of mountains she saw rising over the tops of the buildings across the alley from hers.

They'd always been here. Solid. Protecting. She'd grown up

with them surrounding her, played in their shadow, used the movement of the sun down their sides to determine when it was time to head home.

"I lift up mine eyes to the mountains."

The words of the psalm slipped into her mind, soothing her. The Lord would help her deal with this new problem. Besides, it was only for the next six weeks. Six weeks until she and her mother were gone.

And what would her mother think if she found out about Addison? Could she keep that away from her?

Her heart plunged again, sorrow clawed at her.

She couldn't. She simply couldn't tell her. Her mother had this once in a lifetime opportunity to take part in the therapy that would have her walking again.

And Renee owed her that far more than anything else.

She pushed herself away from the brick wall, forced her stiff lips into a smile, then turned to face Tate and Addison.

"I'm okay," she said, her voice a reedy sound. "I was just feeling faint."

Tate's frown told her he didn't believe her. "You were saying something about a picture?"

"Nothing. It's fine. I just...I haven't been feeling well. Too much stress I think." She gave him a tight smile, then walked past him and Addison, heading to the back room of the scrapbook store, Addison trotting along behind her. "Are we going to finish sorting the pictures?" Addison asked.

How could she do this? How could she look at pictures of her baby in the arms of another woman?

Then her own mother appeared by the table, looking from her to Addison, concern on her features, her hands resting on the arms of her wheelchair. Renee was reminded of the reason she had given up her baby in the first place. "Is everything okay? I saw you running outside."

Renee kept her smile pasted on her face. "Everything is fine. I was just short of air."

Her mother's frown deepened. "Are you sure you're okay?"

Renee wished everyone would stop peppering her with questions. All she wanted was to get through the next half hour without falling apart.

"I'm okay," she said more sharply than she'd intended.

Thankfully, her mother turned her chair around to tend to another customer.

Renee swallowed, her heart still fluttering in her chest. She grabbed the edge of the table, concentrating on the pictures.

They're just pictures, she reminded herself. *Pictures of other people. Don't think of them as pictures of your baby. Addison belongs to Tate. She's not a part of your life.*

"So, let's get these sorted," she said, surprised her voice sounded so normal considering how hard it was for her to breathe.

Thankfully, Addison didn't notice anything wrong and eagerly spread the pictures out, looking over her shoulder at Tate, who had joined them. "You have to help me with this, Daddy," she said.

"Sure thing, sweetie."

In her peripheral vision, Renee caught Tate shooting her another concerned glance, which she chose to ignore. She had a job to do, and Tate was as much a part of her problem as Addison.

The father of her baby.

The man she had unexpected feelings for.

The next fifteen minutes were agony for Renee as Tate and Addison sorted through the pictures, chatting about various things, consulting Renee as to how they should lay them out. And always, in every picture, there was Molly. Blonde, beautiful, smiling. The perfect mother, according to Addison's stories.

The mother Renee never could have been.

"I think that's it," Tate said, laying the last picture on one of the piles on the table. "We don't want the book to get too long."

"Okay. Good." Renee glanced over her shoulder at the clock, then straightened as she turned back to Tate and Addison. "I'm sorry, but I just remembered I have another appointment in about fifteen minutes. So, I don't think it's worth getting started on putting the pictures in the book today."

"Aw. Really?" Addison's wail cut into her heart, but what cut harder was the truth Renee had just discovered. "Can't you change it?"

Renee gave her what she hoped was a regretful smile. "Sorry, sweetie. I can't."

She caught Tate's puzzled look, realizing how this looked through his eyes. First Renee's initial reaction to Addison. Then the dramatic exit a little while ago. Now she looked like she was brushing them off.

Which she was. Kinsley didn't need to have her go over the printing of her potential photography brochures right now.

"If you want, my mother can help you start the book," she said, her mouth growing tired from holding her smile.

Addison pouted as she looked down at the pictures, then shook her head. "No. I want you to help me."

Did the little girl know on some subconscious level who she was? Was that why she was so stuck on having Renee and only Renee help her?

Renee dismissed the questions, her gaze sliding over Tate, who still looked confused. She knew she had to talk to him and explain what was going on, but not now.

Then another thought slipped in.

What would Tate's reaction be to this revelation?

She pushed the question aside, as well. For now, she just had to keep moving. Operate on autopilot and do whatever came next.

"So, we can come back tomorrow?" Addison asked.

Renee tapped her lips with her fingers, making a show of remembering something important. "You know, let me check my appointment book. I think I might have something going on tomorrow after school. I'll call your dad tomorrow and let him know, okay?"

She didn't want Addison's disappointment to influence her, but the little girl's exaggerated pout hooked into her heart.

She glanced at Tate, raising her eyebrows in question.

"Sure. Sounds good," he said, his voice suddenly chilly.

She guessed he knew she was putting Addison off, but right now his opinion of her was secondary to her self-preservation.

He surged to his feet, grabbing his jacket and shoving his arms into it. "C'mon, honey. We should go."

He flicked a hand toward the pictures on the table. "Should we take these along or leave them here?"

"Just leave...them here," Renee stammered, disappointed at her reaction to him. His muted anger bothered her in a way she couldn't examine right now. "They're not a bother."

"Okay. Let's go, Addison. We'll come back when it's convenient for Ms. Albertson."

He'd been calling her Renee until now.

She kept her head down as he and Addison walked past her, realizing how guilty she must look. She managed to hold it together as father and daughter left the store. Then she stumbled to the bathroom and locked the door.

She fought to keep her breath steady, fought to keep the sorrow pushing at the fragile barriers she had spent years constructing against the memories.

Her little girl.

Here. In Rockyview.

Why now?

She swallowed and swallowed and then when she could hold it back no longer, she pressed her hands to her face and wept.

CHAPTER FOUR

"So, that's all we need to do," Tate said, smiling at Tanner and Sabine Bond as they scribbled their signatures on the papers on his desk. When they were done, he slipped a copy in an official-looking folder embossed with the name of his father's law firm on the front. "I'll keep one copy of your will on file here in this office, and this copy is for your own records," he said, pushing the document toward them.

Tanner glanced at his wife, his smile relieved as he picked it up. "So, enough talking about what will happen to Olivia and Courtney when we die—let's talk about life. I'm hungry. How about lunch at Mug Shots?"

Sabine made a reluctant face. "I left Hailey babysitting. I don't know if we should."

"You gave Hailey enough baby bottles to last Courtney for a week. She'll be fine." Tanner dropped his cowboy hat on his head and pushed his wooden chair back, then held out his hand for Sabine. "I guess our next step is to get a safe-deposit box like you suggested."

"Probably a better idea than shoving the will in a box under the bed," Sabine said. She turned her smoky-gray eyes back to

Tate, a dimple flashing as she gave him a quick smile. "On behalf of our two girls, I want to thank you for making this so painless."

"Wills are difficult to think about, but it's important if you have dependents," Tate said, getting to his feet, as well. "If you need anything more, just call me."

Tanner was about to leave, then turned. "I heard you have horses at Evangeline's place," he said. "If you and your daughter ever want to do some riding, we've got some great trails at the ranch."

Tate grinned, surprised again at the wonderful community that was Rockyview. "I think I'll take you up on that. Addison and I haven't had much chance to take the horses out, and I know they're ready for some exercise."

"Just call," Tanner said again. "We'll set something up." Then he turned to Sabine. "So, next stop Mug Shots?"

She laughed, then took his hand as together they walked out of the office.

Tate couldn't help but feel a pang of jealousy at Tanner and Sabine's easy relationship. From the moment they stepped into the office, it wasn't hard to see how much they cared for each other. The way their eyes sought each other whenever Tate had a question. How Tanner's hand rested on Sabine's shoulder. The little smiles they exchanged.

His parents had the same type of relationship, and he'd hoped for the same when he'd married Molly.

The intercom on his phone buzzed, and he pushed the button. "Yes, Debbie, what's up?"

"Are you busy right now? Can you take a quick appointment before lunch?"

Tate glanced at the calendar on his computer. He was free for the next half hour, but he had counted on getting more work done for a local client whose business he was hoping to get. The work would be the nice steady work that was the bread and butter of his previous firm.

But a client was a client, so he said yes.

"I'll send her in," Debbie said.

Tate took his copy of Tanner and Sabine's will and slipped it into one of the large side drawers of his desk. It would go into the vault this afternoon.

However, the her Debbie referred to didn't come in right away. He heard the muted murmur of Tanner's and Sabine's voices from the anteroom, then realized his next client and Tanner and Sabine probably knew each other.

Small towns, he thought with a smile, remembering how the same thing would happen in Whitehorse.

Finally the door opened, and when Tate saw who came in, his stomach dropped.

Renee Albertson. Why was she here?

He steeled himself, trying not to let his concern and frustration from yesterday rise to the surface. Too easily he remembered the disappointment on Addison's face when Renee cut short their afternoon and then canceled their next visit. Obviously she couldn't have been that busy today if she had time to see him now.

Tate smoothed his tie as he stood, politely smiling as Renee entered his office, a hint of her flowery perfume preceding her. "Good afternoon, Ms. Albertson. What can I do for you today?" he said.

In spite of his frustration, he still felt that momentary spark of attraction at the sight of her, which he tried to dismiss as simple loneliness. Renee seemed a complicated woman, and he didn't need any more of that in his life.

Renee twisted her hands together, shot a glance over her shoulder as Tate came around and closed the door behind her. He pulled out a chair for her to sit down, then he went behind his large wooden desk, putting some distance between them.

Renee cleared her throat, then glanced past him at the picture he had on his bookshelf of Molly and Addison. Her eyes rested there, and he caught a surprising wistful look, then she shook her head, as if dismissing it from her mind.

Then her eyes met and held his. He felt as if something momentous was coming.

"Have you...have you heard anything more about the lien?" she asked.

"No. I'm still waiting to hear back from Freddy about setting up a meeting to resolve the issue." Why was she asking this in person? He told her the other day there hadn't been any change. She could simply have called him.

Renee's slight nod acknowledged this comment. "So we wait."

"Yes."

Silence followed, broken only by the muffled tapping of computer keys coming from the outer office and the muted rumble of an engine as a train rolled through town.

Tate looked at her, surprised at the attraction he still felt. As she glanced up at him, he had a sense the pull was mutual.

"I'm sensing there's something else you want to talk about," Tate prompted, leaning back in his chair, trying to dismiss his reaction to her.

"I know that yesterday I seemed a bit...off," she said, her voice quiet. She drew in a slow breath, looking down at her fingers twisted around each other on her lap. "I also know that I wasn't as kind to Addison...to Addison—" Her voice faltered and Renee stopped, as if trying to pull herself together.

She seemed distressed. Then as he watched her struggle to speak, he felt a nudge of sympathy. Perhaps something had happened to Renee in the past? Something that Addison triggered?

But he didn't know what to say, so he waited.

Finally she drew in a long, wavering breath, then looked up at him, moisture glimmering in her eyes. Was she crying?

"When you adopted Addison, who handled the process?" she asked, her question as much of a surprise as her tears.

"Um, actually, it was my father."

Renee's face grew pale, and she fell back against her chair. "Did he tell you who the mother was?"

"No. Only that she didn't want to know anything about Addison. That it was a closed adoption. We were pleased about that because, even though we would have liked to know for Addison's sake, we lived so far up north it would have been difficult to make regular visits."

Renee gave a curt nod, then lifted her chin. "Eight years ago I had a baby girl, born here in Rockyview. Your father handled my adoption, and the only thing I was told about the adoptive parents was that they lived in the Yukon."

Tate could only stare at her, ice slipping through his veins as her words slammed into his chest like physical blows. Eight years ago. Baby girl. Living in the Yukon.

"Are you sure?" was all he could say as questions buzzed through his head, unreal and uncertain.

Renee swiped her fingers across her cheek, leaving a trail of moisture. "What day did you take Addison home from the hospital?"

Tate stared at her, confusion and agitation stealing his voice.

When he'd moved to Rockyview, he'd had a vague notion he might meet Addison's mother, but he had also assumed, because of her desire for a closed adoption, he would never know who she was. Never meet her.

Now she sat across his desk from him. A woman whose life was moving on a path that would take her away from Rockyview.

"What day did you give birth?" he countered.

Renee released a slightly cynical laugh. "I should have

47

known you would prefer to ask the questions. Lawyers don't like to answer them."

Tate suppressed another retort, realizing that his nervousness was making him defensive. So he took a slow breath, then sent up a quick prayer for wisdom and help.

"We picked Addison up from the hospital the afternoon of September seven," he said. "A beautiful sunny day. She was born that morning." His mind slipped back again to that pivotal moment when the nurse had handed them Addison. How he'd felt as if everything in his life had come to such a good place. After the heartbreak of the miscarriages, neither he nor Molly had thought they would ever see this day. A tiny, helpless infant, barely a few hours old, who belonged to them. An infant who would only know them as her parents.

Renee's eyes slid shut and tears slipped down her cheeks as she pressed trembling lips together. "I gave birth the morning of September seven. I left the hospital the next morning. Your father helped facilitate the adoption."

He could only blink as her words echoed in the stark silence of the office.

Gave birth September seven...his father handled the adoption.

He could only stare at her, her words settling into his brain.

The woman sitting across from him was Addison's biological mother.

How many evenings had he leaned over Addison's crib, simply staring at her, letting her fingers curl around his, wondering how someone could have let this precious child go? Sometimes he'd get angry about it. Other times he'd try to understand why. But always, behind all those emotions, he'd felt humble gratitude that Addison's mother had let her go so that he and Molly could take care of her. Could be blessed by her presence in their lives.

"Did you know anything about us?" he asked. "The records

were sealed, but still..." This was Rockyview, and secrets were only kept until they could be shared with someone who didn't know.

Renee sucked in a shuddering breath. "The only thing I knew was something your father let slip. That my little girl, your daughter," she corrected suddenly, "was living in the Yukon Territory. I'd had a bad day. I was struggling with the repercussions of my decision. I knew I had no right...but I came to the office, upset and worried, yearning to know where my baby was. That was all he would tell me. That and the fact that the family was a loving, caring one. I was frustrated but at the same time, I had to accept that nothing could or should change. Knowing she was being taken care of and loved had to be enough for me."

"Molly and I were living in the Yukon when we adopted Addison. I had just gotten a job with a lawyer who was looking for someone to help him out."

Renee nodded, as if absorbing this information. Then, to his dismay, she drew in a shuddering breath.

"I'm sorry," she said, her voice choked as she bent over, picked up her purse and pulled some tissues out of it. She lowered her head, wiping her eyes. Then she looked up at Tate with red-rimmed eyes that tore at his heart. "When did you move to Toronto?"

"About two years after Addison was born." Six months after he found out Molly had cheated the first time. He pushed aside that memory. No sense dwelling on the shame and hurt. "After Molly died, I waited awhile, then came here so I could spend more time with Addison. Working for a prestigious law firm is not conducive to family life." He was telling her too much.

She had chosen to stay out of Addison's life. He had to respect that both for her sake and for Addison's.

Renee dabbed at her eyes. She looked up at him, and again

he felt a connection with her. Had he known, on some subconscious level, that this woman was his daughter's mother?

Or was something else happening?

"So why did you come to see me?" His frustration with his unexpected and unwelcome feelings for her spilled over and he regretted his harsh tone. He unclenched his fists, lowering his shoulders, trying to pull in some calm. "What do you want from me? Are you going to ask for some rights as Addison's mother?"

He didn't relish the idea that now, at this emotionally fragile moment in his daughter's life, her birth mother would make demands.

Renee sniffed again, then waved her hands in an erasing motion. "I don't want anything. Addison is your daughter and I would never confuse her like that," she said. "I don't have any right—" She stopped there, pressing her hand against her mouth.

Relief loosened the tension in Tate's shoulders at Renee's dismissal of his concerns and he sighed. "Okay. I'm sorry I was so short with you. I was worried. Addison has had a lot to deal with in the past year."

Renee looked up, an intensity burning in her eyes even as tears gathered. "I would never do anything to hurt her or jeopardize what you have with her. She's your daughter. You are her parent." In spite of her bravado, her voice broke on the last word, and Tate felt, again, a flash of sympathy for her and the predicament she had found herself in.

But mingled with that was a respect for her integrity.

"I appreciate that."

Renee bent her head and wiped her eyes again. "Sorry about this. It's just..."

"Emotional. I understand, and I'm sorry to have put you through this."

He caught the edges of her smile through the curtain of hair obscuring her face. "You had no way of knowing this would happen. None of this is your fault. You have nothing to apologize for." Then she lifted her head. "I know what my life is like right now. I have my mother and her needs to think about. You know that I'm moving away after I sell the store. So obviously, I'm not going to disrupt Addison's life in any way. She's not to know who I am. For her sake, more than anything."

His respect for Renee grew with each word she spoke. He wondered if Molly would have been half as considerate. "That's kind and giving of you," he said quietly.

She said nothing for a time, letting the silence ease away the emotions of the moment. Then she cleared her throat and crumpled the damp tissue in her hand.

Tate hesitated to ask an obvious question, but knew he had to. "And Addison's father?"

Renee released a cynical laugh. "He's so out of the picture he's not even in the album. He signed away all rights to her. Last I heard, he's married and living in Australia. Dwight was not the type to take responsibility. For anything."

"I'm sorry to hear that."

Renee shrugged. "Don't be. He wasn't worth any of the tears I shed over him." Then she pressed her lips together as if she had said too much.

"So now I want to get to the reason I came to see you. Now that we both know this," she continued, "what are we going to do about Addison's scrapbook? I'm not sure I should continue to keep working with her. I don't know if I can..."

Tate knew she was right, but after the minor fiasco yesterday, all Addison talked about was Renee this and Renee that.

And he felt a kinship with his daughter in that respect. In spite of his best efforts, all he thought about was Renee, as well.

Tate tapped a pen on his desk, trying to see the wisdom in what Renee was saying. "She has her heart set on finishing it. Who could help her?"

"I'd offer my mother's services, but I don't think that would be a good idea, either. My mother is in an emotionally fragile place. One of these days I'm going to have to tell her about Addison, and I'm concerned about her forming an attachment to your daughter right now at this huge turning point in her life. My mother needs to stay centered on what's ahead for her."

"I understand that you hope to enroll her in an experimental program."

"Yes. It's very, very promising but it's...it's costly. And I want my mother to stay focused on that and not be distracted." She bit her lip, worrying the tissues in her hand. "I know it sounds cruel to keep Addison's presence out of her life but right now...right now it will be too difficult for everyone. Not only for my mother but for Addison." She shot him a wry look. "Because in order to tell Addison that my mother is her grandmother, it means telling her I'm her mother."

Once again, Tate was impressed with Renee's selflessness. Last night his father had told him about Renee's dedication to finding a cure for Brenda's injury. How she had been willing to give up the store that had been her dream to see that come through. All that made her even more appealing to him.

A conundrum to be sure.

"Let me tell you how much I respect you for your consideration. I'm sure this isn't what you envisioned when you gave Addison up."

She pulled in a quick breath, glancing up at him, a yearning look on her face that hooked his heart.

"You don't have to answer if you don't want to, but has she ever asked about...me...about her biological mother?"

Tate held her troubled gaze, puzzling what to tell her.

"She's been curious, of course, but I have tried to emphasize the fact that we chose her. That we wanted her. She knows she didn't come from the stork—" he released a light laugh, trying to ease away the sudden tension in the room. "She has wondered, for sure. I expect that will come out more in time."

Renee nodded, her mouth curving in a gentle smile. "I'm sure she'll be curious." She paused and Tate wondered where she was headed next. He said nothing. Waiting to see where she would go.

Renee cleared her throat. "For now, we have the scrapbook to deal with. One option would be for me to put together a kit for her with some instructions. That way she could finish it on her own. With your help."

Tate leaned back in his chair, his arms folded across his chest, biting his lip, trying to find the best way to respond to this. "That could work. However, she seems to have formed a deep connection with you. She's not going to like—"

The door of his office suddenly burst open, and Addison bounded inside, her backpack swinging from one hand.

All color drained from Renee's face, and she clutched the arms of the chair with a white-knuckled grip. Then she drew in a breath and forced a smile to her face.

And Tate realized how hard it must have been for Renee to see his daughter initially. She hadn't known who Addison was the first time they met in the store, but maybe, on some biological level, she felt a kinship. A connection.

Now her actions made far more sense, and he felt a pang of sympathy for her.

"Hey, Renee. What are you doing here?" Addison asked, tossing her backpack on the table in the corner and coming to stand beside her, her eyes glowing with pleasure.

Tate's heart dropped to his stomach as his gaze flicked from Addison to Renee and then back again. He saw a resemblance between them where he hadn't before. They had the same heart-shaped features. The same slightly slanted eyebrows. The same coy half smile that could melt his heart...

Renee's cheeks flamed, and Tate saw she was struggling for self-control. He had to help her out.

"So...why are you here so early, Addison?" he managed to get out, fully aware of the heightened emotions in the office. "Aren't you supposed to be in school?"

"Nope. It's early dismissal today. I told you yesterday. You probably forgot," Addison said, bouncing on the tips of her toes as she often did when she was excited. Her entire attention was focused on Renee, however. "So, can you still help me with my scrapbook?" Addison asked, clearly unaware of the tension in the office that she'd walked into. "You said you had to do something today, but you're here now."

Renee shot an agonized appeal for help to Tate, and his brain scrambled to find something to say to his daughter.

"Miss Albertson still has an appointment," Tate said vaguely. "In fact, Miss Albertson just found out she'll be so busy she won't be helping you with your scrapbook anymore."

Addison's mouth dropped open, looking first to Renee, then to Tate. "Why not?" she whispered.

The ball was in Renee's court now.

"Um. Well, I'll be busy getting my store ready to sell," Renee said, improvising. "And, um, we have a lot to do before we go."

"I won't be in the way," Addison said, her shoulders slumping, her head drooping. "I'll be real quiet. I just need a bit of help."

"Maybe your dad could help you," Renee said, trying to sound reasonable, but Tate heard the anguish edging her voice. "This way, just the two of you can work on it. It will be a special time."

"He was coming to the store because he doesn't know nothing about making a scrapbook," Addison protested, turning to her father.

"Addison," Tate warned.

"Well, you don't," Addison said, her lower lip trembling. "And I wanted Miss Albertson to help us because her mother said she couldn't help me and now nobody can. I really want to make this book for my mom. Because I miss her so much and I don't want to forget her and I don't want you to forget her and if you don't help me and if Miss Albertson doesn't help me, then everyone will forget her." Addison stopped, her head lowered, her shoulders shaking, her face scrunched up in an expression of utter sorrow. Then the tears started up.

"Oh, honey," Tate said as he got up, hurried around the desk and folded her into his arms. He held her close while she sobbed against him, glancing over her head to Renee, whose own eyes glistened with tears. "We won't forget her. We can work on it together. I promise."

"You won't. You're always so busy and you never have time and you won't have time for this and I'll have to stay every day after school in this stinky office and the book won't turn out nice at all." Her words tumbled out, broken by sniffing and hicupping.

Okay, Lord, I'm going to need some divine guidance here, he prayed.

He stroked her hair some more, feeling utterly helpless. He had obviously underestimated how much Addison still missed Molly.

Molly is the only mother she knows, Tate thought. Then he looked over at Renee.

What was he supposed to do about this?

CHAPTER FIVE

Don't give in. You can't give in.

Renee clenched the tissue in her hands while the sound of Addison's sobs wrenched at her heart.

She couldn't look at Tate, who was watching her as if wondering what she would do.

You're leaving. You can't get involved with these two. Addison was her daughter, and Tate, well, Tate was another problem altogether. Now that he knew who she was, she couldn't let herself be involved in their lives. It wasn't fair to Addison.

Or Tate.

And yet, as the girl continued to cry, Renee's heart softened. The part of her that always wondered what it would have been like to keep her. The part of her that imagined an alternate life with her daughter, wondering what kind of things they would do together rose up. Taunting her.

She's my daughter. My little girl. What would be so bad about spending time with her?

The thought made her heart skip a beat, and she blamed that reaction on what she said next.

"You know, Addison, if it's that important to you, maybe I

56

can find some time to help you with the book," Renee said, the words tumbling out of her before she could stop them.

Addison sniffed, then lifted her head away from Tate, as she swiped at her wet cheeks. "Really?"

Renee caught her gaze as second thoughts swirled in her head. She knew this would just make everything more complicated. She tried not to look at Tate to catch his reaction to the situation.

You gave her up. You have no right to be in her life. Especially because you're leaving.

The other voice, the accusing voice rose up, the words like a fist to her chest. But at the same time, she knew this was one thing she could do for Addison. For her daughter. Though her mother was her top priority, Renee could help this sad girl capture the memories of her adoptive mother.

"Really," Renee assured her, her voice shaky with a mixture of emotions. "But we have to make sure it doesn't take too long because I still have to sell the store."

"Not right away."

"No. Not right away."

"And my daddy is going to help."

Tate hesitated and Addison shot him a frown.

"Daddy, please, you promised."

"Yes, I'll help," Tate assured her.

Renee caught Tate's glance as he said this. She wasn't sure how to read him, but she would be lying if she didn't feel the tiniest thrill of anticipation at the thought of working so closely with him every day.

"You promise?" Addison asked.

Renee nodded, her smile growing at the sight of Addison's beaming grin.

"Yay! I'm so happy!" Addison turned to her father. "We're still going to make the book!"

Tate's expression was reserved, and Renee sensed he wasn't

entirely sure this was a good idea. But for Addison's sake, they had to find a way to make this work.

"Are you still busy today?" Addison asked her. "Can we start today?"

Tate jumped in to help. "Actually, sweetie, we got a few things sorted out for Miss Albertson, so, yes, I think she can help you today."

Renee gave him a grateful smile, then turned her attention back to Addison, whose grin threatened to take over her face.

"So I guess I'll see you both soon?" she asked.

"Give us about half an hour?" Tate asked.

"That should work."

Tate's gaze held hers, and again she felt the connection between them. She knew she had to ignore it.

It was just a mixture of loneliness and being around an appealing guy, she reminded herself. She would have to be careful as they worked together. She just hoped this scrapbook wouldn't take too long to finish.

⟨⟨⟨∘⟩⟩⟩

"AND THIS IS when Mommy and Daddy and me went to Disney-land the first time." Addison held up a picture of a beautiful blonde woman hugging Addison, who looked to be about three at the time. "Mom is so pretty in this picture."

Renee looked up from the Disneyland stickers she was sorting out for Addison to use in her scrapbook and couldn't help but agree. Molly had been a stunning woman. Tall, blonde, with an easy elegance that shone through in every picture no matter what she was doing or what she wore. In a few of the pictures Molly and Tate stood side by side, and Renee had to admit they were a striking couple. A perfect family for her little girl.

"She is very pretty," Renee said, struggling to keep the wistful tone out of her voice. She knew it would be difficult helping Addison with her album, but she didn't think it would be this hard. Every time Addison and Tate talked about a trip they'd made or drives they'd taken, Renee compared what Addison's life would have been like had she kept her.

No trips to Disneyland. No shopping excursions where Addison would come home with enough toys to keep four girls happy.

Every memory they shared was a reminder that Addison had ended up in a better home than any Renee could have provided as a young, single mom. It comforted her yet created an ache of melancholy.

Though Renee felt vindicated in the choice she had made for Addison, regret still clawed at her.

While she struggled with her own emotions, she wondered what Tate was going through as Addison laid out the pictures on the large craft table they had taken over in the back of the store. Was he missing his wife? Did seeing pictures of her make him sad?

As if he knew she was looking at him, he raised his eyes to catch hers, but she didn't see sorrow in them. She saw something more troublesome.

Attraction.

The same thing she felt every time she saw him.

"Look, Renee, here's me on Splash Mountain. See how scared I look," Addison said. In the photo, Molly sat behind Addison, holding her close, laughing herself.

"You do look scared," Renee agreed, dragging her attention back to the pictures.

"Screamed like a little girl," Tate said, giving Addison a one-armed hug.

"I was a little girl," Addison protested.

"And that's why you screamed like one."

Addison grinned, looking down at the picture. "So, what do we do next?" she asked.

"Now we decide how to lay out these pictures on this page. Maybe your dad can put them in order, and we can figure out what colors to use to make them stand out and how many other things to put on the page. You should also leave a space for writing a story about the pictures."

"There's some red in each of these pictures," Tate said, setting out four pictures on the page. "Why don't we go with that color? What do you think, Addison?"

She nodded, agreeing with her father's choice. Tate had a good eye for color combinations, which surprised Renee. More than that, he was infinitely patient with Addison, who got distracted every time a new customer came into the shop.

"I like red, but I like purple better. Just like Renee."

Renee smiled at that. "What was your mom's favorite color?"

"Green."

Tate and Addison spoke at the same time, then they chuckled and bumped fists. A little routine Renee was sure they didn't even think about.

"But not a dark green. More like water in a lake?" Addison looked at her dad for reassurance.

"I think it's called aqua, and please, no comments about how I know the name of that particular color," he said, shooting Renee a smile.

"When you start rhapsodizing about the difference between eggshell and cream, I'll start wondering," Renee returned, pulling the paper cutter toward her, thankful for his humorous comments that eased the tension between them.

The buzzer rang and she looked over her shoulder just as the door fell shut behind Evangeline.

"I'll be right back," Renee said, jumping up. She didn't want Evangeline coming into the back room and seeing Tate or

Addison here. Her friend would be curious and would start asking questions laced with innuendo.

"So we just stick the pictures in now?" Tate asked.

"Unless you want to mat them first."

"I'm sure my fellow lawyers will be impressed that I know how to mat a picture as well as what embellishing a page means."

"Just wait until we start with the glimmer mist," Renee retorted, determined to keep the tone light.

"I don't even want to know." He caught her grin and returned it with one of his own.

That little curl of awareness that his smile so easily created tightened in her stomach.

She spun around and hurried out of the room. As she came around the stickers aisle she almost collided with Evangeline.

"Doing a card class?" Evangeline asked, looking past Renee to the back room.

"No. Just helping a customer put a scrapbook together." Renee took Evangeline's arm and led her to the front of the store. Evangeline was kangaroo quick when it came to jumping to conclusions, and after their conversation at the book club about Tate, Renee was fairly sure where Evangeline would land. "What did you want today?"

"I sold out of all those bookmarks you made me and was wondering if you could print up some more." Evangeline trailed behind Renee, still shooting questioning glances over her shoulder. "As well, I saw the brochures you printed up for Kinsley Tye. They are gorgeous. I was thinking I might want something like that done as well."

"Sure, but can we talk about that another time?" Renee didn't want to take Evangeline to the back where she had the computer she worked on to set up the graphic mockups. "As for the bookmarks, how many do you want?" Renee asked, making a note on the pad of paper she always had by the phone.

"About a hundred."

"Can do," Renee said, pulling out her order book and writing it up.

"By the way, have you had a chance to read the book I picked for Book Club? Mia was wondering what you thought."

Renee shook her head. "No can do. If I tell you now, you'll text her right away. I'm saving my comments for book club. Otherwise we won't have anything to talk about."

"As if that ever happens," Evangeline said with a wry note.

Renee laughed, then caught a movement behind Evangeline. Oh, no. This was not good.

"Renee, I think we're out of glue," Addison announced, holding up the glue container. "My daddy said he's no mechanic, so he can't fill it up."

Renee stifled a groan as Evangeline looked at Addison with a gleam in her eye. "I'm guessing your daddy is Tate?" she asked.

"Yep. He is," Addison answered. "Tate Truscott. Renee is helping me and my dad make a scrapbook. Of my mom."

"Really." Evangeline drew out the single word, loading it with innuendo as she shot Renee an arch look. "That's kind of her."

"One hundred bookmarks," Renee said, ignoring her friend's cheeky grin. "When did you need them?"

"Soon as possible, though if you're busy..." Evangeline let the sentence fade away as she added an exaggerated wink.

"Not busy at all." Renee tried to sound in charge and competent but her response to Tate and Addison had thrown her off kilter and she was pretty sure Evangeline noticed.

She certainly didn't need her friend stirring the pot.

"I'll be with you in a flash," Renee told Addison as she ripped the paper off the pad and tucked it into her to-do file.

Addison nodded, then trotted to the back of the store, leaving an intrigued Evangeline leaning against the counter, watching her go.

"I thought her mother was dead?" Evangeline said.

"She is, but the scrapbook is Addison's way of remembering her."

"Addison is adopted, isn't she?" Evangeline asked.

The word sent a shot of adrenaline through Renee.

"Yeah, she is."

"Interesting that Tate chose to bring her back here," Evangeline said, looking back at Addison, then at Renee.

Renee shot a panicked glance at Addison's retreating back, feeling as if the fact that Addison was her biological daughter was stamped all over her face. Feeling as if the similarities between her and Addison were there for everyone to see.

Evangeline knew every detail of Renee's life. Knew exactly how old her baby would be. What if Evangeline put everything together? What if she took her deductions to Mia?

Somehow she had to distract her friend from the situation. Addison could not get even a hint that Renee was her mother. It would be devastating for her so soon after her adoptive mother's death and her move here.

Plus, Tate would think she had something to do with the disclosure.

Renee grabbed at the first idea that dropped into her head. "Well, I'm glad Tate did," she said, adding what she hoped was a sweet smile. "And Tate has been great about helping her put the book together. In fact, I suggested that he work with her, and I'm so glad he agreed." She blinked her eyes, hoping, praying Evangeline's romantic heart would home in on the diversion.

"I thought you weren't interested in Tate?" Evangeline said, her own grin dimpling one of her cheeks as she leaped to exactly the conclusion Renee wanted her to.

Bingo.

"Well, you know, he is attractive, and I guess I'm just a weak woman," Renee said, relief sluicing through her as she put on a fake, simpering smile, embroidering on the situation.

Evangeline gave Renee a satisfied smile. "Well, you sure change your tune quickly."

"Not so quickly," Renee said, suddenly wishing she hadn't started down this road. "But I'm taking it slow," she said, giving herself a vague out. "I still have my plans in place."

Evangeline nodded, her expression suddenly serious as the implications of Renee's plans settled in her mind. "Of course, but who knows what can happen once you get back?"

"That's a long ways away," was all she would say. Her mother's therapy was such a huge time commitment she had never thought past that.

"It's amazing what you're doing for your mother," Evangeline continued, toying with the card at the till. "But sometimes I wonder if you haven't made too many sacrifices. Given up too many dreams. I know you love this store, and you and your mother have done such great work here. But Tate seems like a great guy. I'd hate for you to lose your chance with him."

Even as Renee felt guilty, her eyes slipped past Evangeline to the room where Tate and Addison worked.

Tate glanced up and caught her eye, his smile tipping up one corner of his mouth, highlighting a shadow of a dimple.

Even from this distance he made her heart trip. For a tiny moment, possibilities hovered with tantalizing promise.

Then the front door of the store opened. As her mother entered, the whisper of her wheelchair swept away the momentary delusions.

❧❦❧

"THIS DOESN'T SEEM RIGHT," Tate grumbled as he followed his father down the streets of Rockyview, the warm afternoon sun shining down. Though it was still early May, spring was heralding its approach in the greening of the trees in the town, which spread up the mountains reaching to the dark green of the spruce and fir trees and the snowcapped tops.

"What doesn't?" his father asked, nodding a greeting to a passing couple.

"Heading out to lunch on a Monday morning without a client in tow," Tate said as they walked up the steps to Mug Shots. "Doesn't seem professional."

"Get used to it," his father said, pulling open the door of the coffee shop. "In a town like Rockyview, it's good business to frequent the local coffee shops."

Any comments Tate might have had were carried away by the jumbled noise of the café as they stepped inside. Jazz music wafted from speakers, adding to the rumble of conversation filling the space. Customers lined up alongside the glass display cases, which held a surprising variety of sandwiches, croissants, bagels, muffins, cookies and pastries. People jostled for seats at tables as waitresses in black shirts and pants scurried from the kitchen delivering the hot food people had ordered at the counter.

The place was hopping.

A woman in a pink bandanna bustled in, sliding trays of premade sandwiches, wraps and bagels into the display case and barking out orders to the two young men at the grill.

While Arlan and Tate took their place in line, the woman in front of them turned around. Her bright eyes and white permed hair were set off by the vibrant blue of her velour jacket and pants. The blinding-white running shoes were wishful thinking. Tate doubted the older woman did more than amble in them.

"Arlan, this must be your son," the woman said, gesturing toward Tate. "He looks just like you."

"Tate, this is Sophie Brouwer. One of our clients," his father said with a smile that underlined his previous comment about client contact.

"I'll need to talk to you about updating my will now that my son, Ben, is married," Sophie said.

"I heard. Congratulations," Arlan said as the line moved.

"Jennie Bond and I had a hand in bringing him and Shannon together, you know," Sophie said, lowering her voice as she leaned closer, her bright button eyes glowing with pride. "We have a bit of a matchmaking reputation," she said, turning her attention to Tate, as if he might be interested in enlisting their services.

He gave her a vague smile, hoping she didn't see that as encouragement.

"Tate's wife died not that long ago," his father said to Sophie, putting his arm around Tate's shoulders.

"Of course. I understand," Sophie said, placing her hand on Tate's arm in a gesture of sympathy. "But if you ever need to talk to someone, we're available."

The only reply Tate gave her was a quick nod. Then, thankfully, it was Sophie's turn to order.

The young girl at the cash register gave Sophie a wooden spoon with a number on it. Sophie took her change, dropped it in the pot by the cash register and, after waving in Tate and Arlan's direction, headed directly for a table by the window where another older woman was motioning to her.

"That was...interesting," Tate said, turning his attention back to the chalkboard with the day's menu written on it. "Nice to know that the women of this town have my interests at heart."

"Oh, she's not the only one," Arlan said as he pulled out his wallet. "You're considered quite a catch."

"Plenty of menu choices for a small café," Tate said, preferring to ignore his father's comment. Though his father wasn't as overt as Sophie Brouwer, he had, from time to time, made comments that one bad experience shouldn't sour him to all future relationships.

Trouble was, it had. He had misjudged Molly so badly and

been so betrayed by her actions that he didn't trust his judgment. Thankfully, it seemed Addison hadn't suffered any long-term repercussions from a marriage that had been crumbling. And working on the scrapbook seemed to show her that Molly had, at times, been a loving mother.

Once they received the soup and sandwiches they'd ordered, his father took the tray and wove through the crowded tables to the large French doors open to the patio. "Thought we'd eat outside," he said as he stepped through the doors. "Not as crowded."

Tate didn't care either way. He just wanted to eat and get back to the office. Saturday he'd taken Addison out to the ranch to see the horses, and Sunday he'd gone to church with his father. Though weekends off was probably a normal occurrence for his father, Tate was still adjusting to the concept.

"Doesn't look like there's any place to sit here, either," Tate said, glancing around the crowded tables.

But his father ignored him, and when Tate realized where his father was headed, he almost groaned aloud.

Renee sat at a small wooden table, leaning close to her mother, the sunlight glinting on the waves of her caramel-colored hair. Her hands fluttered as she spoke, emphasizing a point she was making. Brenda laughed and Renee joined in, the sound settling in Tate's soul.

He couldn't help but think of the steady litany of complaints that had personified Molly's relationship with her own mother. He couldn't ever remember her laughing with her mother, let alone having lunch with her or working with her.

Or making the sacrifices Renee was willing to make for her own mother.

As his father drew closer, Renee's mother looked up, and her smile widened as her hand brushed her hair away from her face. "What a pleasant surprise," she said, glancing from Tate to his father. "Why don't you two join us," she said, pointing to the two empty chairs at their table. "We have lots of room."

Tate guessed, from the faintly smug look on Mrs. Albertson's face and his father's hasty agreement, that this was a setup.

What was his father doing? He of all people, knew exactly who Renee was.

However, that was forgotten as they settled themselves at the table. Tate was far too aware of Renee sitting across from him. Her blue-and-orange-flecked nail polish, a whimsical touch for someone who seemed so practical, sparkled in the sun as her restless fingers fiddled with the locket hanging from her neck.

His father and her mother were chattering away like old friends, but Tate's mind went suddenly blank.

Tate took a spoonful of soup, wishing he didn't feel so awkward in her presence. Though they had already spent a couple of afternoons together, there existed a curious discomfort between them. He knew part of that unease had to do with the fact that Renee was Addison's biological mother.

Tate would be fooling himself if he didn't admit that another part of the awkwardness had to do with the struggles he was dealing with. Renee was a beautiful woman, a caring daughter and faithful friend. Where did she fit in his life?

Then, as he looked over at her, their eyes met. Tate knew he should look away but didn't want to.

Her eyes were an intriguing mix of green and brown bordering on hazel. Her lashes were thick, and her eyebrows had an intriguing arch to them, emphasizing her heart-shaped face.

Just like Addison's.

Reality lumbered into the moment, and Tate dragged his gaze away.

"And how was your weekend?" she asked, her quiet voice startling him. "I understand you went out to Evangeline's ranch to ride?"

"How did you know?" he asked as he sprinkled salt into his soup, trying to keep himself busy.

"Evangeline told me." She gave him a self-conscious smile. "I don't mean for you to think that we were gossiping. It's just, well, she's one of my best friends. We talk a lot."

"I guess that's all part of small-town life," he said. "Gotta get used to that."

"And if you're not careful, whatever you say here will get passed around by way of the Mug Shots Messaging Service."

"The what?" he mumbled around the food in his mouth.

Renee waved her arm toward the people gathered on the outside deck. "This place always has people coming and going. They talk, they share information, and it spreads all over town."

Tate laughed. "Actually, the day at the ranch went well. Addison is getting better on her horse. I'm hoping to take her out on a longer ride soon. Tanner offered to let me come to his ranch and ride the trails."

"That sounds like fun."

"Do you ride?"

"Evangeline and I would take our chances on the horses her father occasionally brought to the ranch. I wouldn't call it riding as much as hanging on."

"Sounds risky, riding unfamiliar horses."

Renee laughed. "We were young and foolish and had the usual dreams preteen girls have about horses. That they wanted to be our friends." She shook her head as she brushed some crumbs off the table beside her plate. "Just one of the many silly notions young girls have."

Her voice took on a plaintive note, and he wondered if she was referring to Addison's biological father. Though she had told him what he needed to know, he caught himself wondering at the relationship.

And if she'd had any since then.

"Addison seems to have the same romantic view of horses

you do," he said. "She doesn't realize that horses are a friend that could easily kill you with one well-placed kick."

"Now there's a lovely thought to carry with you next time you go near a horse," she said with a chuckle.

Her laughter was infectious and Tate joined in, easing the tension between them. They grew quiet, then Tate's attention was caught by his father's laugh.

"Are you sure that's how it happened?" Arlan was asking as he leaned closer to Renee's mother.

"Have I ever lied to you?" she returned.

Tate watched them a moment, confused at the flirtatious tone in Mrs. Albertson's voice. And his father's. Tate hadn't seen him smile like that since his mother died.

What was this all about?

He caught Renee glancing at her mother, then at him, her expression as quizzical as his.

"Are you seeing what I think I'm seeing?" he asked, leaning closer and lowering his voice.

"I'm not entirely sure what you're seeing," she returned, her voice equally low and filled with confusion. "But I'm starting to understand why she insisted on sitting at a table for four." Renee turned her head toward him at exactly the same time he looked at her.

Their gazes connected. Held. And as Tate looked into her eyes, he felt as if his soul was slowly drifting from its moorings. For a moment he let himself wonder about him and Renee.

Then he drew back and clenched his fists. He couldn't do this. Couldn't allow himself to get pulled into Renee's life.

"With both you and your mother here, who's minding the store?" Tate asked, bringing them back to reality.

"We have a girl who comes in to help us from time to time," Renee said, pleating her napkin. "She also comes in every Monday to work the lunch hour so my mother and I can have our lunch date." Renee turned away from him, toward her mother. She reached over and laid her hand on her mother's arm.

The action was so natural it produced a twinge of melancholy in Tate. Renee had a warm, loving relationship with her mother that, for a moment, made him miss his own mother.

"Look at all of you, so cozy and precious," a voice called out from the sidewalk running alongside the patio.

Tate heard Renee groan, then turned to see who was talking. Evangeline, her long wavy blond hair flowing over her shoulders, waved at them, her other arm clutching a large manila envelope.

"Hey, Evangeline," Renee said. "Tate and his father joined us for lunch."

"I can see that," Evangeline said, the gleam in her eyes making Tate wonder if he was missing something. "Did you have a good horseback ride?" she asked him.

"I did," Tate replied. "Addison enjoyed it, as well."

"Awesome. Glad that worked out for you." Evangeline glanced from Tate to Renee and winked at her.

What was that about?

"Don't you have books to inventory? Shelves to stock? Reviews to post online." Renee asked.

Evangeline held up the manila envelope. "Just got back from the accountant. Need to mail out the ranch's and bookstore's year-end stuff for my dad to sign."

"Well, then, you better get to the post office," Renee said, a surprisingly stern note in her voice.

Evangeline just laughed, grinned at Tate, then flounced off, the full skirt of her dress flowing behind her.

Tate was truly mystified. He glanced back at Renee, who looked apologetic and was about to say something, when his father called his name.

"Tate, we're not busy on Mother's Day, are we?" he asked.

"I don't think so."

"Great." Without any further explanation, his father turned his attention back to Mrs. Albertson.

Okay, his father was up to something. And Tate was convinced it had as much to do with him and Renee as it did with, what it seemed to him, his father and Renee's mother.

Trouble was, Tate wasn't sure how he felt about it all. He glanced at Renee, and when she smiled at him, his own confusion grew. He reminded himself that Renee had her own plans, and they didn't include sticking around Rockyview.

He wasn't going to put his daughter, or himself, through that kind of emotional turmoil again.

CHAPTER SIX

"So, you didn't come by yesterday," Renee said as Addison and Tate settled themselves at the table in the back of the store.

Tate didn't meet Renee's eyes as she chatted with Addison. He knew his excuse for not coming yesterday had been lame. Truth was, he'd needed breathing room from Renee Albertson. Their little "lunch date" on Monday had been too enjoyable. He had found himself thinking too much about her afterward. Wondering about her. Remembering her smile and how appealing she was.

"My daddy said he was too busy." Addison pouted at Renee. "But I got to go to a friend's place. Her name is Talia." She turned to her father. "Remember when I told you that Talia wasn't helping me?"

"Yes, I do."

In fact, Tate had been surprised Addison had agreed to visit her after she had assumed her friend didn't like her.

"She said that Natasha doesn't get Math Facts and that our teacher asked her to help Natasha. That I was good enough at

Math Facts and didn't need help. I felt bad that I was mad at her. She still wants to be my friend and I said she can.

"Well, I'm glad you got that sorted out," Tate said.

"Me too. I feel bad that I was mad at her." Then she tipped her head to one side, smiling at the page she had just finished. "I like this page, don't you, Daddy? Me and you and Mommy had fun on this trip."

"Yes, we did," Tate said, thankful that Addison's memory of that day didn't mesh with reality. He and Molly had had a huge fight that day, and, for Addison's sake, he had tried to keep a fragile peace.

"Looks like you and your mom and dad went on lots of great trips," Renee was saying, bending over the pictures Tate was sorting. "Where were these taken?"

"Toronto Island," Tate said, forcing his attention on the pictures. "You liked that adventure," he told Addison, trying to ignore the scent of Renee's perfume as she stood between him and Addison.

Addison smiled and nodded. "I remember we went swimming and Mommy pushed you into the water. I laughed and laughed when you got your pants and shirt wet."

Again Tate was thankful for her innocence. Molly had pushed him off the dock because she was angry with him, her erratic behavior becoming increasingly troubling.

"But it was a warm day, so I dried off quick," he added.

"And then we went biking on those fun bikes that four people can ride, except just Daddy and Mommy biked. I got to sit and look at the fun little houses there."

"That sounds like a good time," Renee said. "So, what do you want to add to this page?"

"I think we should just keep this page simpler than the other ones we did," Tate said, laying the pictures of the bike trip out on the empty page of the scrapbook. "We need to get this book done on time."

Addison frowned as he pulled out the tape dispenser. "On time for what?"

"Um, Mother's Day, of course, and that's in four days." He pulled that deadline out of nowhere, and he saw from the puzzled look Renee shot him that she also wondered why there was a rush.

"But Mommy's not here," Addison said, flipping through a couple of sheets of stickers.

"Well, don't you think it would be kind of special to have it done by Mother's Day anyway?"

"Kind of."

"I think that's a good idea," Renee added, as if guessing at his reasons, as well.

Tate shot her a grateful look. Her careful smile told him she seemed to be feeling the same as him.

"Hello, everyone."

A female voice snagged Tate's attention. A petite, dark-haired woman stood in the doorway of the craft room. Her short hair enhanced elfin-like features. She glanced from Tate to Renee with a speculative gleam in her brown eyes and a pair of dimples flashing from her cheeks.

"Oh, no," Renee breathed, holding her hands up to the woman as if in warning. "Hey, Mia, Mom's out in the store if you need anything."

"Oh, I don't need anything. I was just talking to Evangeline." The woman named Mia looked from Renee to Tate and then back again, grinning. "Thought I would come and see what you're doing."

"I'm making a scrapbook of my mommy," Addison said helpfully. "Do you want to see?"

Tate caught Renee's look of dismay and wondered what seemed to be the matter.

"I would love to," Mia said, pulling out a chair beside

Addison as if ready to settle in. "Why don't you show me what you've done already."

"Addison and Tate are busy," Renee said, catching Mia by the arm before she sat down. "As, I'm sure, are you? Who's minding the flower shop?"

"Oh, don't you worry about my business," Mia said. "But I'm curious about yours?" Mia gave her a broad wink and a flick of her head in Tate's direction.

Renee rolled her eyes, then tugged on Mia's arm. "And you're busy, too. I think I see someone going into the flower shop."

"Blythe is there. I'm just taking a break from a big order from Hidden Creek Inn," Mia said, her dark eyes focusing on Tate and Renee as if looking for something. "Larissa and Garret are having some fancy shindig there. Something to do with some bigwigs from the government and other sawmills for Larissa's dad."

"That's great," Renee said, walking toward the door, practically pulling her friend along with her. Considering that her friend was only a few inches above five feet and Renee looked to have about six inches on her, it wasn't much of a contest.

"Guess I'll be seeing you around," Mia said, pointing to Tate and adding a bright smile, flashing her dimples again.

Then they were out the door, and Tate turned his attention back to helping Addison, making quick work of putting the photos down on the page.

"Now we have to write something about the pictures," she said, pulling the cap off a colored pen.

"We can do that at home. Let's just get the pictures done first," Tate said. He wanted to get this book done. Wanted to get away from the confusing distraction Renee was causing in his life.

Renee came back a few minutes later looking flustered. She glanced over her shoulder, then back at Addison. "My mom said she has some new stickers to show you, Addison. Do you want to see?"

"Were those the ones I wanted?" Addison asked, dropping the pictures she was holding.

"They certainly are. My mom is at the front of the store with them."

"Yay!" Addison bounced off the chair, knocking the pile of remaining pictures onto the floor.

Tate blew out a sigh, then bent over to pick them up just as Renee reached for them, as well. Their fingers brushed, and Renee snatched her hand back.

"Sorry about that," Tate muttered, his own fingers tingling with reaction. "That kid has the attention span of a gnat sometimes."

"She's doing really well," Renee said, getting to her feet and straightening out the supplies lying on the table, fussing with the scraps of paper. She shot another look behind her, then turned to Tate, her expression serious.

"I sent Addison away for a few moments. I...I feel like I should explain something." She sighed and folded her arms over her chest. "Mia and Evangeline...I'm sure you're wondering about their strange behavior the past few days. It's just...they're...well..." She paused, her one hand wavering in the air as if trying to capture the words she labored to get out. "They seem to think that we're an...an item."

Tate looked baffled. "Item?"

"They think I'm interested in you." Renee lifted her shoulder in a self-conscious shrug as her words registered with Tate.

To his own surprise, he felt his heart give a juvenile thump.

"It started when Evangeline stopped in last week." Renee moved closer, lowering her voice. "Evangeline has always been at me about trying to find out where my daughter...well, Addison...was. She's a romantic at heart and seemed to think that it would be good if my daughter found out who her biological mother was. I never wanted to mess up my daughter's life like that, as you know." Renee stopped, blew out her breath as she plunged her hands through her hair in a self-conscious gesture. "This is a small town. News travels. Evangeline already knew that Addison was adopted. So when Addison came up to the desk to ask about the glue container the other day, Evangeline was staring at her. When she started asking questions about Addison, I got nervous, and to deflect her questions about Addison, I sort of, well, made it sound like...we...you and I..." Renee let the words hang between them, a flush working its way up her neck.

"Sorry, I'm not sure what you're getting at," Tate said with a light frown.

"I made it sound like I was interested in you. That the reason I was working with you and Addison was because it was a way to spend time with you, not help Addison." Her words tumbled out as the pink in her neck reached her cheeks.

Tate stared at her, her last words surging around the small space they occupied.

"That's why Evangeline made those comments the other day at Mug Shots," Renee continued. "And that's why she went hotfooting to Mia, who, of course, had to come here to see for herself. Ever since you came to town, they've been joking about what a perfect couple we'd make and we both know that can't happen, but I made it sound like it could."

Renee's last words came out in a rush followed by a heavy sigh, as if she was glad to be free of them.

But even as what she said registered, the fragments of conversation, the arch looks and the heavy hints all became crystal clear.

"I was wondering what Evangeline was talking about at Mug Shots," he said. "And that's why Mia was looking at me with that look just now."

"Exactly." Renee dragged her hands over her face. "I'm sorry if I made you uncomfortable. I did it to distract Evangeline from Addison. I was so worried she would put two and two together —" She stopped there, looking behind her again.

Her concern for Addison's well-being touched him. He guessed it wasn't easy for Renee to admit all this, or to even distract her friend the way she had. In spite of her discomfort, he admired her selflessness.

"I'm really sorry if I made you uncomfortable," Renee repeated. "My friends mean well, but they can get carried away. Especially Evangeline. She's such a romantic." Renee shook her head and blew out another sigh. "I just hope she hasn't been blabbing to our other friends."

Tate laughed at the dismay on Renee's face, surprised he didn't mind. "Don't worry about it. I think my dad has been thinking the same thing your friends were."

Renee shot him a look of horror. "Has Evangeline talked to him?"

Tate held up his hands in a placating gesture, smiling at the look of dismay on her features. "I have a feeling that's how we ended up sitting together at Mug Shots the other day. So don't worry about your friends, because I think my father is on the same wavelength."

Renee released a nervous laugh. "Oh, boy."

"Oh, yeah."

Suddenly self-conscious, they exchanged a quick glance, then their gazes broke apart.

She probably thought her little speech would release some of the tension between them, but instead, Tate found himself more aware of her than before.

He sneaked a quick look at her, to gauge her reaction, and caught her looking at him, too.

"So, I guess we need to figure out how to get around this," Tate said, knowing they needed to deal with this, yet feeling a curious reluctance to be realistic and practical. "I mean, you'll be leaving soon and—"

"I don't want Addison to find out about me."

Tate nodded. They were being mature and responsible. Nothing could begin between them.

"Maybe I could tell Evangeline that it just didn't work out," Renee suggested. "You and me. That would keep her brain going in the right direction."

"You mean, you're breaking up with me?" Tate placed a hand on his chest, injecting a note of humor into the situation.

Renee's bubbling laugh made Tate smile even more.

"It could have been such a happy-ever-after." Renee sighed dramatically, playing along. "Just the type of story Evangeline loves."

Tate laughed again, and in that moment, as their eyes met, he felt a flutter of disappointment that puzzled and confused him even more.

The file on his desk dealing with the builder's lien against the store was a reminder of Renee's future.

Addison's presence a reminder of Renee's past.

"I just hope Evangeline can stay distracted until we get this scrapbook done," Renee said, growing serious again. "We can't let Addison find out."

"Let me find out what?"

Tate's heartbeat faltered as Addison skipped into the room, holding a package of stickers.

His shocked gaze flew to Renee, who stood there, hand pressed to her lips.

"Um, can't let you find out about the surprise," Tate said.

Addison just laughed. "I already know about the surprise."

"You do?"

Tate and Renee spoke at the same time, and Addison giggled. "Now you have to fist bump," she said, looking from one to the other.

"That's you and your dad's thing," Renee said, her hands clasped in front of her, her eyes riveted on Addison.

"It could be your thing, too," Addison said with a grin.

Tate knew Addison wouldn't let it be, so he made a fist and reached across the table. Renee hesitated, then at Addison's urging, made a fist herself. They bumped, their eyes met again, and Tate felt his heart quicken.

Then Renee pulled her hand back.

"So tell me what you know about the surprise," she asked, wrapping her arms around her midsection.

Addison giggled again, her hand over her mouth, shoulders hunched. "That Mrs. Albertson has something special for me when I finish my scrapbook."

Relief sluiced through Tate as he caught Renee's puzzled look. Obviously she was as confused as he was.

"Then we have to hurry," Renee added, sitting down at the table beside Addison. "We have only a few more pages before Mother's Day."

To Tate's surprise, Addison nodded, grabbed a couple of pictures and laid them out on the page. "We can use these stickers, okay?" She held up the package that Tate suspected Mrs. Albertson had given her.

Tate nodded, and the next half hour zipped by as Addison, inspired by whatever it was Mrs. Albertson had said, devoted herself fully to the task at hand.

"Will we get it done tomorrow?" Addison asked as she cleaned up the scraps of leftover paper.

"Maybe not tomorrow, but certainly the day after that."

Addison nodded. "That's good, because Mother's Day is on Sunday. And that's when—" She stopped, her hand flying to her mouth as if to prevent what might come out.

"That's when what, honey?" Tate asked, slipping the pictures that hadn't been mounted yet in a colorful box Renee had provided.

Addison giggled and shook her head. "Can I go look at some more stickers before we go?" Addison asked.

"You just looked at some stickers. Besides, it's almost closing time," Tate said. "And you need to help us clean up."

"I'll be quick." And she ducked out before he could stop her.

"Sorry about that," Tate said, feeling a need to apologize for Addison's flightiness.

"She got a lot done in the last half hour," Renee said as she stacked up the papers.

"That was mostly thanks to you," Tate said quietly, dropping the pens into the bucket Renee had set out. "I really appreciate how you managed to keep her on task. She's so distractible."

Renee laughed, tapping the papers straight. "Apparently I was the same way when I was a little girl." She cut him an apologetic glance as she dropped the papers, her eyes wide. "I'm sorry," she said. "I shouldn't have—"

"Don't worry about it," Tate said with a gentle smile. "It's to be expected to see some similarities."

Renee's smile held a hint of melancholy. "I do, but I don't want to intrude."

"You haven't. And I want to say how much I appreciate your tact and consideration. I'm sure this can't be easy for you."

Renee fussed with the papers on the table, avoiding his gaze, but he caught a hint of a smile teasing one corner of her mouth. "It isn't, but at the same time, it's cathartic for me to know she ended up in such a good place, with such a good mother and father. I'm sad for her that she lost Molly, so I feel like this is one thing I can do for her before I go. Help her document her memories of Molly."

She looked up at him, and Tate's heart twisted as Renee's sincere words coupled with the truth of who Molly really had been.

He wanted to blame his heightened awareness of her on

loneliness, but in his deepest heart he knew something else was happening between them.

And before he could stop himself, he closed the small distance between their hands and covered hers with his. He squeezed and she returned his touch.

"So there you are." Renee's mother appeared in the doorway, glancing from Tate to Renee. "Addison said you were still here."

Renee snatched her hand back, and Tate looked away, hoping Addison hadn't caught that little exchange. Thankfully, Addison didn't show up, too.

"Are you two done here?"

"Yes. Just cleaning up," Renee said quietly, her voice holding the faintest tremor. She shook her hair away from her face and shot her mother a quick smile. "Where's Addison?"

"Still looking at some stickers she wants for the book. Ashley is helping her." She looked behind her, then wheeled herself farther into the room. "Tate, I understand you're looking to buy a house here in Rockyview."

Tate was momentarily taken aback at her comment. "I am. Addison and I have been staying with my father long enough. I want to settle here. Make a home here."

"If you're in the market, our house is for sale."

Renee frowned. "I don't know if Tate would be interested—"

"Of course he would." Mrs. Albertson looked back at Tate. "It's a beautiful home. My husband was a carpenter, and he fixed it up. It has a large backyard, and the house is big enough that, if you want more family, there's plenty of room. We had it listed, but our real estate agent didn't do much for us, so we decided to try to sell it ourselves."

"Well, sure. I guess I could look at it." He had checked out a few houses with a real estate agent, but hadn't found anything that caught his eye.

"We're going to need the money if this store doesn't sell,"

Mrs. Albertson was saying. "I think you would love it, and if you buy the house, it would save us both real estate fees. And you're a lawyer, to boot," Mrs. Albertson said as if everything was already settled. "Why don't you come by on Saturday?"

"Sure, I think that could work." His father could look after Addison.

"Perfect. We'll see you then."

Then she spun her wheelchair around and left.

"Um, are you okay with this?" Tate asked Renee after Mrs. Albertson had gone. "Me coming to look at your house?"

"Of course," Renee said, waving off his objections. "It's just a house, and the reality is, like my mother said, we're going to need the money now more than ever if I can't get the lien off the store in time."

"It'll happen," Tate assured her. He had set up an office appointment for Freddy and Benny to discuss the situation. He was fairly sure they could come to an agreement.

"I really appreciate what you've been doing about the lien," Renee said quietly as they finished cleaning up. "It's been a needless complication for me."

"I'm sure you have enough on your mind," Tate said, returning her careful smile, then he glanced down at what was left of the pictures. "And from the way Addison worked today, looks as if we might get this scrapbook done by Mother's Day after all."

"I think that would be good."

It wasn't hard to hear the faint note of relief in her voice. "I want to say how much I appreciate your willingness to do this for Addison," Tate said, straightening the box of pictures, shifting the papers to one side. He looked up at her, holding her gaze.

Renee looked away.

Tate caught the faintest glimmer of a tear in one eye and felt like smacking himself.

"I'm sorry," he said, lifting his hand to touch her elbow. "I shouldn't have said anything. I didn't mean to upset you."

Her only reply was a curt nod as a tear tracked down her cheek. She turned her head and swiped at it with a surreptitious movement.

But as he left, he gave her arm a gentle squeeze, fighting the urge to pull her into his arms and comfort her.

It was definitely time to go.

❦❦❦

RENEE GLANCED AROUND THE HOUSE, wiping her suddenly damp palms down the legs of her blue jeans. She should have worn a skirt and shirt instead of jeans and a hoodie.

Then she wondered why she cared. She wasn't a real estate agent trying to make an impression on a client. She was just a woman trying to sell a house.

To a guy you're attracted to and the adoptive father of your daughter.

Renee wished, for the hundredth time, that the next few weeks were behind her. Wished that she and her mother were in Vancouver, getting ready for the therapy sessions.

Seeing Addison every day was like a white-hot agony. How many times had she stopped herself from reaching out and brushing the little girl's hair away from her face? How often had she dragged her attention away from Addison's happy face to the project they were working on?

Yet she couldn't deny her feelings or change them. Even worse, Tate was woven into the whole business. He was the father of her daughter. A good man, and way more appealing than he had a right to be.

Renee grabbed a pillow and pounded it, taking out her frustrations on the innocent object. She looked around the house again with an assessing eye.

Should have decluttered more, she thought, remembering too late the frequent advice she heard on the TV shows she loved to watch. She walked to the fireplace to remove some of the pictures on the mantel, when a knock on the door stopped her midstride.

Her eyes flew to the grandfather clock tucked in a corner of the living room. Tate was ten minutes early.

She glanced around one more time, stifling the crazy beating of her heart at the thought of Tate in her house, then strode to the door and yanked it open.

Tate stood at the top of the step, looking away from the house, a smile fixed on his face, a lingering scent of soap wafting toward her.

Then he turned to Renee, his deepening smile enhancing the strength of his chin.

He was way too attractive for his own good.

"Was just looking at the view," he said quietly. "I love the location of this house. Up on a hill like this."

"That's why my dad bought it," Renee said. "I'm so used to it I don't always notice, but it is beautiful."

She was babbling. Yanking the front door all the way open, she stood aside. "Come on in."

Tate glanced over his shoulder again, then stepped into the house.

"So, obviously this is the living room," Renee said as she watched Tate's appraising glance flick around the entrance. "When my dad bought it, he had plans to put on a front porch, but after my mother's accident we needed to make the house more wheelchair accessible, so we added a ramp, and now there's not really room for a porch. It would be nice to have one, because there's not much space for boots and such unless you go through the back entrance."

Again. Stop with the chatter.

Tate didn't seem to notice, however, as he stepped farther into the house. "How many square feet is the place?"

"About eleven hundred on the main floor. There're two bedrooms on this level, three rooms upstairs and a basement that we haven't done much with."

"Looks homey," Tate said, his hands shoved into the pockets of his blue jeans. "I like how the living room flows into the dining room."

"My dad did some renovations. He took down a couple of walls to open up the space."

"I like the hardwood floors."

"I do, too. They're especially wheelchair friendly."

Tate pointed to the fireplace. "Does that work or is it just for show?"

"My father put an insert in it, so, yes, it is a functioning fireplace." She followed him as he walked over to it, suppressing the compulsion to rearrange the pictures on the mantel. In one on the far left she was obviously pregnant. Renee had kept the picture as a small way of acknowledging the baby she had borne for nine months.

And as a reminder of the consequences of the poor decisions she'd made in her life.

"How old is the house?" Tate asked.

"It was built in the twenties. My dad rewired it to bring it up to code. Put insulation in the attic and retrofitted the outside with new siding."

"You know a lot about the construction of the house," Tate said, giving her a grin.

"Every day after school I'd stop by, pick up a hammer or nail gun and work beside him," Renee said. "One summer, I had thoughts of becoming a carpenter."

"But you started a scrapbook store instead."

Renee nodded. "I loved helping my father, but I love playing around with paper and glue way more. The store grew out of a hobby my mother and I shared."

"Sounds like you had a good relationship with your parents."

Renee gave a wistful smile as she looked around the house. So easily she recalled laughing with her father as she held boards for him to saw, handed him nails and ran a hundred little errands. "I did. My father was a loving, patient man. Took me a while to get over his death."

"What happened to him?"

"He died of lung cancer about ten years ago. He smoked like a steam engine. I was angry with him because of that." She stopped herself. Why was she telling him this? She hadn't talked about her father in years.

Tate held her gaze, frowning.

"The dining room is over here," Renee said, moving past him, trying to regain control of herself, dismayed at the memories deluging her after all this time. "My father also put in the bay window by the dining-room table and put in new kitchen cabinets."

Renee walked around the island that held an eating bar with three stools that were only used the times Mia and Evangeline would come over after book club.

"I like the stained-glass lamps," Tate said, pointing to the set of three small lamp shades suspended over the eating bar. They were red with a pattern of leaves twining around them. Simple but beautiful.

"A woman named Naomi made them a couple of months ago," Renee said as she flicked the switch to make them come alive. "My mother gave them to me as a birthday present."

"Would they come with the house?" Tate asked.

Renee felt a flicker of guilt as she switched the lights off, knowing she would have to leave this particular gift behind. She remembered how pleased she'd been with the surprise and how she loved the way they shone in the evenings.

"They would have to," she said, turning away from them to the rest of the kitchen. "My mother and I will be renting a place in Vancouver. So I can't bring them along."

"That's too bad," Tate murmured.

"The appliances are older, unfortunately." Renee waved a hand toward the fridge and stove, surprised at the emotions creeping into her mind. It was as if showing Tate around this house made her realize how much of herself she had invested in it and how much she would be leaving behind.

Don't think about that. Think about what will happen for your mother.

Those thoughts centered her, and she managed to push the doubts aside.

"You might want to look at replacing them in a couple years. The cabinets are over ten years old now but still in excellent shape."

"They look great," Tate said, running his hand along the countertop. "Your dad did quality work."

"He always told me that if you're going to do something, do it right or don't bother." Renee smiled as she remembered her father's often-repeated advice.

"I wonder if your dad and my dad went to the same school," Tate said, opening and closing one of the cupboard doors. "He says the same thing."

"Your dad is a good lawyer and a wise man." Renee's gaze caught Tate's. Awareness seemed to buzz between them. Renee wanted to dismiss it as merely attraction to a good-looking man, but her heart told her different. Working with him and Addison had shown her other aspects of his personality that were as appealing as his blue eyes and his strong features.

He was a good father and a good husband. A solid person and, as her father would say, a good man to have beside you in a storm.

She was realizing that she couldn't do this. She didn't have space in her busy, complicated life. And he was a problem with no easy solution.

But even as her practical mind told her one thing, her heart, her lonely, yearning heart, pleaded with her to do another.

CHAPTER SEVEN

*L*ook away. Stop right now.

"So what does the rest look like?" Tate asked, dragging his attention back to the house with an intense effort.

"My mother's bedroom is on the main floor. I sleep here, as well." Renee waved her hand to the back of the house. "Did you want to see the rooms? We've had to change the bathroom for my mother, but I'm sure that can be changed back."

Was it his imagination or did Renee sound as breathless as he did?

Please, Lord. Help me to stay focused. And in control.

He clenched his fists as he drew in another steadying breath.

She is the biological mother of your daughter. It's too complicated.

But even as that thought stormed through his mind another followed.

How easy would it be? A relationship with the woman who gave birth to your daughter? It would be such a natural progression.

"It's okay. I don't need to see the bedrooms," he said, dismissing the idea. He was in her house, looking to buy it because she and her mother were moving away. He could dream all he wanted but Renee was focused on her plans. It wouldn't be right to confuse her and it would be selfish of him. "I wouldn't mind seeing the basement and the upstairs, though."

Renee went ahead of him up the narrow stairs that led to the second floor. He glanced behind him before following her up. The house was homey. Cozy. Renee and her mother had made it welcoming and friendly.

He couldn't help but compare it to the modern apartment Molly had chosen for them when they'd moved to Toronto. Cold and austere and expensive.

"We haven't done much up here," Renee was saying. "My dad had plans of fixing these rooms up, as well. But that didn't happen..." Her voice trailed off as she opened a door to a room off the narrow hallway at the top of the stairs. "This is the sewing room."

Tate walked past her and looked inside. A few chairs stood along the wall, a chest was pushed up against another and a dressmaker's dummy was parked in one corner by a table that held a sewing machine.

"Do you sew?" he asked.

"My mother did."

Again he heard that muted note of regret in her voice, and again he thought of all the things that had changed not only for Renee but also for Mrs. Albertson after the accident.

He walked across the hall and inspected the other room, smiling at the view the large window afforded him. The space beneath the window was taken up by a long table covered with scraps of paper, stamps and ink. A few completed cards hung from a metal stand at one end of the table.

"Do you work here as well as at the store?"

"Sometimes at night I like to craft. Gives me something to do if my mother is tired."

"Have you always done this? Work with paper?"

"All my life. My mother said if she wanted to get me out of

her hair, all she had to do was give me some scissors, paper, glue and crayons."

"Now you can play with all the paper you could want."

"I still get excited when we get a new shipment in," Renee said with a smile as she straightened a pile of paper, her hands lingering. "It's not the only thing I do, though. I've also branched out into graphic design. Designing and printing up logos, brochures, wedding invitations. It's been a natural progression for my business. But my first love is cutting and gluing."

"I imagine it will be difficult to give up the store when—" Tate held up his hand as if stopping himself. "Sorry. I don't need to underline what you're dealing with."

Renee gave a melancholy smile. "It will be hard, but I believe it'll be worth it."

Silence followed that admission. Then Tate walked out of the room, moving on to another topic.

"I guess I should look at the basement, as well, and pretend I know something about foundations and dry rot and termites," he said, leading the way down the stairs.

Renee's gentle laugh warmed his heart. It was good to hear her laugh. She didn't do it too much.

"I can't help you there," she said as she walked past him to a door across from the kitchen. "I know as much about basements as I do about electronics."

She flicked on a light just inside the door, and he followed her down the worn, wooden stairs.

"This is the part in the movie where the spooky music starts," Tate said as the stairs creaked under his feet when they descended into the cool, damp basement.

"At least we don't have to walk in the dark to pull on a string attached to a lightbulb," Renee added.

"But the humming of those fluorescent lights does add to the creepy ambience," Tate said, glancing around the large, open space. "I'll just walk around and frown, and tap on floor joists and look knowledgeable, and then we can go back upstairs where it's safe," Tate said, his voice echoing in the cool space.

"Frown away," Renee said, a note of humor in her voice.

Tate did walk around, envisioning what could be done down here. One corner of the room was taken up with a furnace and hot-water tank. The walls had new insulation but hadn't been drywalled. The floors held markings of what, he suspected, were future walls. Obviously Renee's father had plans for this that hadn't come to fruition.

He returned to where Renee stood at the bottom of the stairs. "I guess that concludes the tour," he said with a grin.

"Unless you want to see the backyard."

"I've seen enough to know this is a prime piece of real estate and easily worth whatever you and your mother are asking."

"You don't even know the price," Renee said, leading the way up the stairs.

"Don't need to," he said. "I just moved from Toronto. Anything here is a bargain compared to the prices there. But you might want to talk to your lawyer first."

"You are my lawyer."

"Then you're in a tough situation. We might have a conflict of interest happening here."

"Why don't I make a cup of coffee and we can work on the interest and the conflict thereof," she said, taking the pot from the coffeemaker and turning on the tap water.

"Sounds like a good idea." Tate didn't mind sitting down with Renee for a while.

He slipped his hands in his pockets as he walked to the bay window overlooking the huge yard. Flower beds flanked by a wide flagstone walkway stretched along the fence on one side of the yard. A cluster of tall trees shaded one corner. A wooden swing attached to rope hung from their overhanging branches. Some chairs sat beside a fire pit in the shade of the trees. Tate could easily see Addison playing in the large, fenced-in area. In Toronto, all she'd had was a small balcony. She would love it here.

The coffeemaker burbled as Renee set mugs out, then put together a plate with cookies and brownies. His mouth watered at the sight. They looked homemade.

"How do you take your coffee?" she asked as she filled his mug.

"Just black," he said, pulling out two chairs. "Adding cream and sugar to my coffee wastes billable time."

"I guess every second counts," she returned with a smile as she set the pot on the counter. "But I'm not going to counter with any lawyer jokes. I still need you to get the lien off the store."

"I understand the buyer is getting antsy. Do you think she's still interested?"

"I hope so. She was the only one who replied to my ad."

Tate felt a flash of sympathy at the anxiety in her voice. He knew what was on the line for her with the sale of the store and, in an unguarded moment, reached over and covered her hand with his.

When he felt the warmth of her hand, he regretted his impulse, but when her fingers twined around his, all reservations fled.

"Could you rent the store out? Get someone else to manage it?" he asked, wishing he could help her with more than advice.

Renee shook her head, still holding his hand as if his touch anchored her. "I need everything I can get my hands on to pay off the loan on the store, and pay the bills for the treatment and living expenses for the year and possibly longer if things don't go as well as we hope—" Her voice broke and she pressed her lips together, cutting short whatever else she might have said.

Tate was quiet a moment, letting her gain control. "This is

quite a sacrifice you're making for your mother," he said quietly. "You're an amazing daughter."

"I'm far from an amazing daughter," she said.

"That's not true. I see how attentive you are. How caring. I can't think of anyone who would be willing to give up their home, their job, their career for the sake of their mother's health like you are."

Renee slowly shook her head. "It's no sacrifice. It's payment."

"What do you mean, 'payment'?"

Renee's silence drew out the tension. She said nothing more, but Tate felt as if he was on the verge of discovering something important.

"What kind of payment?" he asked, encouraging her to speak.

Renee pressed her lips together as if holding back the words, then with a gentle shake of her head, she spoke. "I'm the one who put her in that wheelchair."

"What do you mean?"

Renee pulled her hands away from him, twisting them around each other. "I was the one driving when the accident happened," she continued. "The accident was my fault."

Her words fell like stones, taking with them anything he might say. All Tate heard in the heavy silence following her shocking confession was the faint tick of a clock, the hum of the refrigerator.

He dug through his mind, trying to find some way to comfort her, to take away the pain that laced her voice, but he knew anything he said would come across as trite and meaningless.

So he simply laid his hand on her shoulder in assurance and, he hoped, solace.

He waited a moment, then spoke. "Do you want to talk about it?"

"I try not to." Her words came out slowly, weighted with

sorrow. "It hurts too much to think about it, let alone talk about it."

"I think it might help if you did."

She shook her head. But Tate knew that even the most reluctant witness would often speak to fill a silence. So he waited.

Then after a long, slow intake of breath, she began, her voice pitched low and quiet. "I was in a bad place in my life. My boyfriend, Dwight, and I had been partying pretty hard. I was wasting my time in college, not living the life I should have. I'd turned my back on God and my mother. Not good." Renee released a bitter laugh. "We were in the car together, fighting about that. Fighting about what I was going to do about...about Addison. About Dwight. I told her to mind her own business. Then we came to a tight corner on the road..." She faltered, and Tate tightened his hold on her shoulder.

"I wasn't paying attention to my driving. The road was wet, and because I was so focused on trying to convince her I was right, I didn't make the corner. The car swerved and I drove it over a steep embankment. It landed on the passenger side. My mother...she was...she was injured and I—" She stopped there, turning her head away from him, her gaze fixed on the window. "I was okay."

Her knuckles were white. "I can still hear my mother screaming in pain. Still feel the helplessness of not being able to take it away." She drew in another shaky breath. "It seemed to take forever for the ambulance to come. I was fine, my baby was fine, but my mother wasn't."

Tate was confused by her comment, then came the shocking realization.

"You were pregnant when the accident happened," he said quietly, his hand moving over her shoulder.

She nodded, her eyes straight ahead. "We were arguing about the baby when I drove off the road. My mother was trying to persuade me to keep the baby, telling me that she would help me take care of her. I wanted to give her up for adoption. Dwight had left me. He didn't want any part of a baby in his life, and I knew I couldn't take care of her the way I should." Her lip trembled and tears coursed down her cheeks, glistening in the light from the window. She hastily brushed them away, shaking her head, releasing a harsh laugh. "Sorry. Don't know why I'm so emotional about this now. It happened nine years ago."

Tate heard the anguish in her voice and guessed the reality of having Addison in her life now brought back memories from that time.

She swallowed and continued, "Dwight had left me, and I really couldn't take care of myself, let alone a baby. But my mother really wanted a grandchild—" Her voice staggered to a halt. She took a quick breath then continued, "When I found out the extent of her injuries, I knew there was no way Mom could help me take care of a baby. She would need me to care for her full-time. So I gave her...I gave Addison up." She stopped there, covering her face with her hands, her shoulders shaking. "I'm sorry," she said, stumbling over the words. "I'm sorry."

The air was thick with loss and sorrow, and Tate couldn't sit by idly anymore. He shifted closer and pulled her gently into his arms.

He said nothing, just held her as her sobs built in intensity, racking her body, and her tears dampened his shirt.

His heart broke for Renee and the difficult choice she'd been faced with, the sacrifice she'd made for the sake of her mother.

"You don't have anything to apologize for," he said, raising his hand to stroke her damp hair away from her face.

But she kept crying, her anguished sobs tearing at his heart. He rocked her gently, stroking her hair, whispering quiet encouragement as he helped her navigate this storm.

Please, Lord, he prayed, help me find the right words to say to this sorrowing woman. Help me to do the right thing for her.

Because right now, in spite of his own misgivings, he didn't want to let her go. She felt so right in his arms. Like she was meant to be there.

And the longer he held her the more right it felt. She seemed to fill an empty space in his life that had always been there.

Until now.

❦❦❦

RENEE WANTED to stop the tears and grief pouring out of her like waves. But it washed over her, mocking the self-control she had struggled to shore up from the moment she'd found out about her mother's injuries. From that moment, she'd known she had to choose between her mother or her baby.

Tate's arms around her created a haven and, as the sorrow subsided, a shelter she didn't want to leave.

His voice murmured into her hair; his hands stroked her arm, soothing and comforting. Strength and security.

Her head felt hot and achy, and slowly she became aware of the dampness of Tate's shirt. From her tears. She made a token effort to pull away from him, but his arms tightened around her.

"It's okay," Tate whispered, his hand pressing her head back into the crook of his neck.

So she kept her eyes closed, letting herself drift against him and the sanctuary of his arms. *Just a few more moments*, she promised herself. Just a few more seconds of letting someone else be strong for her. She'd had to carry so much in the past years, it was a blessed relief to just rest against the solidity of Tate's comfort. To let someone else offer their strength, their support.

To feel a man's arms around her.

Tate's arms.

Even as her heart yearned to stay in this refuge, her practical mind told her that letting him hold her like this would complicate her life and cloud her decisions.

She curled her fingers against his shirt, her eyes closed.

Just a few more moments. A few moments of support and comfort.

But finally she drew on the self-control she had clung to all these years, wiped her eyes one more time, then pulled away. She pushed her hair back from her face, her eyes swollen and sore from shedding tears she had suppressed for so long.

Tate kept his hand on her arm, clearly as reluctant to let her go as she was to leave.

"When was the last time you cried?" Tate asked finally, his fingers making gentle circles at the back of her neck.

Renee wiped her eyes with the heel of her hand. "When the nurse walked away with Addison in her arms."

"All that time." Tate's voice held a note of wonder. "All that time you've been strong, and held in your sorrow," he continued. "Was there no one to comfort you?"

Renee swallowed down another sob, wrapping her arms around her waist. "Mom was unconscious in the hospital, and my friends all had their own difficulties."

Mia was dealing with a shaky marriage. Evangeline had been dealing with a broken heart. Renee couldn't burden them with her sorrow. Her aunts and uncles and grandparents had come to visit, but they all lived far away and couldn't offer ongoing support.

Her guilt over what had actually happened, over how her mother had been injured had kept her from telling them the truth.

Tate trailed his hand along her arm, creating a light shiver that danced down her spine.

"It was during that time that I returned to my faith," Renee continued. "I couldn't have gotten through it otherwise. So I really wasn't all alone."

"I know what you mean," he said, his gaze still holding hers. "There were many times in my life when I thought I could manage on my own, but learned, especially after Molly died, that God's strength carried me through when I couldn't."

Tate's eyes shone with a conviction she knew to be true. As his words settled into her heart, she felt as if one more barrier was broken down between them. They shared a faith in a God who had brought them both through difficult times in their lives.

Possibilities hovered on the periphery of her mind, and she felt the quickening of her awareness of him. She couldn't look away; didn't want to. Her world had narrowed down to this moment with this man.

She didn't know who moved first, him or her, but it seemed the most natural progression for their lips to touch. Their arms once again to embrace.

She moved closer, her hand holding his neck, his tangled in her hair, anchoring her close.

His lips were warm, soft, inviting. With a moan she moved her mouth over his, tasting him, inhaling the masculine scent of him.

Her heart raced and her thoughts narrowed down to this moment. This man.

It felt so right.

And Renee didn't want it to end.

Finally, slowly, Tate drew away, letting his forehead rest against hers.

His breath was warm on her cheek. She closed her eyes, letting the moment sink in.

Visions of Addison, her mother, his father floated in her mind but she pushed them aside.

Not yet, she thought, reveling in the moment. It had been so long since she was held by a man. Seen as desirable. But this wasn't just any man. This was Tate. Someone she had allowed to come closer to her than she had ever let anyone since Dwight.

The memory of Addison's father was like a sluice of cold water.

Behind memories of him was an onslaught of other obligations and responsibilities and she slowly withdrew from his arms.

He eased out a gentle sigh, trailing his finger down her cheek. "You are so beautiful," he said. "In so many ways."

His words kindled a yearning she hadn't allowed herself to feel since Dwight left her. A yearning for someone to see her as a person who had nothing to do with caregiving or work. A yearning for someone to support and sustain her when she couldn't handle things on her own.

Then the phone's sharp ring intruded. She glanced at the display before she picked it up. It was her mother calling from her cell phone.

As always, she felt a stab of worry as she hit the talk button. "Hey, Mom, are you okay?"

"Of course I am. Why do you always ask me that?"

Because I always worry about you. Because you are in a wheelchair and anything could happen if you're not careful.

"Because you don't always call from your cell phone, and I know you're out and about."

"And I'm fine," her mother said with a surprising sharp tone in her voice. "Stop fussing."

Renee pressed her lips together to hold back a retort. "Why did you call?"

"I just thought I'd let you know that I might be a little late. I'm still at Sophie's place, but the wheelchair lift in the van was acting a bit jerky, so I've called Jack Dilton, the mechanic, to come have a look at it while I'm still visiting."

"It's probably that loose connection again." Renee glanced at the clock, surprised to see it was already nine. Her mother liked to be in bed by nine-thirty.

"No. No. I'll wait for Jack."

"I'm coming right away."

"I thought Tate was there to see the house."

Renee turned away from him, unable to face him right now, feeling as if her mother could sense his presence, would know what had just happened.

"Oh, we're done here," was all she said as she got up from the chair.

"Okay, then. How did it go?"

"Um...yeah, good." Renee didn't want to talk about 'how it went' because so much else had happened. "But I'll come right away." She ended the call and set the receiver on the little stand by the back door. Her mother's dilemma brought her back to her senses and her priorities.

"Is there anything I can do?" Tate asked.

Renee appreciated the offer, but answered, "No. Thank you. I know what needs to be done."

"Are you sure? I don't mind."

"No. It's just a simple fix. I'll have to get after Jack and get that done properly."

"Wow. A paper crafter, businesswoman and mechanic," Tate said with a note of admiration.

"A girl's gotta do what a girl's gotta do," she said with a dismissive wave.

Tate laughed as he glanced around the house one more time, as if assessing it as he picked up his coat.

Then he looked back at Renee. "So you're sure about selling this place?"

Renee felt her own convictions waver. Was she sure?

A few weeks ago there was no doubt.

But now?

"I have to sell it. For my mother," she said with more force than necessary, as if she had to eradicate the kiss they had just shared, bring herself back to reality.

His curt nod indicated that he understood. Probably more now than he had before.

"Of course you do," he said, his eyes taking an inward look. He tossed his jacket over his shoulder and hesitated for another moment, as if still unsure of her decision.

Renee felt her breath quicken as questions hovered between them. His smile held a hint of sadness, then he turned and left.

As the door closed behind him, she leaned against the wall nearest her, needing the support.

Her fingers floated up to her mouth as if to feel the kiss they'd just shared. Then she heaved out a breath of frustration. The kiss had been a colossal mistake. It could never happen again. She had to keep her distance from him. He was too complicated and tempting.

Why, Lord? she thought, closing her eyes. *Why did You bring him into my life? This can't happen.*

Yet even as she tried to convince herself, the memory of their kiss lingered.

CHAPTER EIGHT

*T*he doors of the church elevator creaked open, and Renee pushed her mother out and into the back of the foyer. The noise of people chatting washed over them as Renee negotiated the gathering. Just as they came to the open door leading to the sanctuary, a young girl, Natasha, skipped over to them, her brown ponytail bobbing behind her, her gray eyes sparkling and her hands full of brightly colored carnations.

"Happy Mother's Day," Natasha said, her wide smile taking in both Renee and Mrs. Albertson. She handed Renee's mother a red flower and gave Renee a quick smile, then skipped off to give a flower to another mother, obviously pleased with her duty.

Renee held back a prick of sorrow as her mother sniffed the flower. Mother's Day had always been difficult for her. Each year the day was like pressing an unhealed bruise.

This year, however, it brought a poignancy and pain that hit even harder. This year, the daughter she had given up had come back into her life.

Renee negotiated her mother's chair past a group of people

laughing and chatting, and wheeled her into their own special place in the church sanctuary.

Years ago, after her mother had come home from the hospital to stay, Benny, a local carpenter, had shortened one of the wooden pews so Mrs. Albertson could park her wheelchair beside the pew and not block the aisle.

Renee sat down, and as she scanned the bulletin, looking for news, a movement in the aisle caught her attention. She couldn't stop from looking up any more than she could stop her heart from beating.

Tate and his father walked down the aisle of the church, Addison between them, holding both their hands. She was about to look away, when Tate shot her a quick glance, and Renee felt her resolve crumble like a cracker.

They settled in a pew one ahead and across the aisle. Renee looked away from the man who had starred in her thoughts all night and the little girl who had been ever-present in her dreams.

But this little girl's father had kissed her, and had thrown Renee's life into a tailspin she was trying, desperately, to recover from.

Then, as the service started, Pastor Blacketer congratulated all the mothers in the audience and commended them for their love and sacrifice on this important day.

Unable to stop herself, Renee's eyes slid over to where Tate and Addison sat. Addison waggled her fingers at her, grinning. Something elemental stirred in Renee's chest.

She shifted her concentration from them to the tasks she had coming up. She had to call Freddy about the lien, Cathy Meckle, the buyer, confirm the conference call, look into flights to Vancouver and try to confirm the sale of the house.

Even as the litany of her responsibilities swirled through her head, she could still feel the kiss Tate had given her. She had felt a deep connection with him.

Pastor Blacketer announced the opening song, and she rose to her feet with the rest of the congregation, looking over to the words on the screen.

"My Jesus, my strength, my rock and solid fortress, my hope, my song, my light in the wilderness."

She sang with the congregation, letting the words draw her along, reminding her of where her hope and her strength lay. This song had comforted her those long days after she had walked out of one hospital alone, then stood vigil beside her mother's hospital bed. Those days when life seemed bleak and dark, devoid of hope. Thoughts of Jesus had been like a shimmering light of promise, holding her and her mother up.

To her dismay, she suddenly felt the sting of tears at the backs of her eyes. She clenched her fists, focusing on the words. She couldn't cry again. She wouldn't.

After last night, it was as if the dam had broken, and her sorrow was threatening to overwhelm her again. Last night had been a moment of weakness she couldn't allow to happen again.

Dear Lord, help me to stay on task, she prayed. *Help me to put my needs aside and to focus on my mother's.*

Slowly she felt the sorrow subside, and as she sat down, she kept her eyes fixed on the pastor, letting his message soak into her weary soul.

However, by the time church was over, she felt the beginnings of a headache pounding at her temples.

After the last notes of the last song resounded through the church, Renee put the songbook down. She wanted nothing more than to go home, put her feet up and lose herself in the book Evangeline had chosen for their book club. She didn't care that it was a historical romance, complete with a dashing earl and a feisty debutante.

But just as she grasped the handles of her mother's chair to wheel her down the aisle, they were joined by Arlan Truscott.

"Good morning, Renee," he said. Then he smiled down at her mother. "Happy Mother's Day, Brenda."

"Thank you, Arlan."

"I was wondering if you and your lovely daughter would like to join us for lunch," he continued. "As a way of thanking you both for all the work you have done on Addison's scrapbook. She's so proud of it."

Please, no, Renee wanted to cry out, but then Addison joined them.

"Can you come? Please?" Addison pleaded, grabbing Renee's hand, her little fingers clinging to hers. "That was the surprise I wasn't allowed to tell you, but I kept it a secret, even from you, Daddy."

"Good job," Tate said, smiling.

In spite of the emotions roiling around her soul, she started to voice her regrets, when her mother spoke up, cutting off her protest.

"We'd love to come," Brenda said. "We don't have any other plans."

Had her mother forgotten the casserole Renee had made and the cake she had baked for their own Mother's Day celebration?

"That would be wonderful," Arlan responded, glancing back at Renee. "Then we'll see you there."

And that, it seemed, was that.

But as Renee pulled out of the church parking lot, her foolish heart couldn't stop the zing of anticipation at the thought of spending more time with Tate.

❦❦❦

"THAT WAS AN AMAZING LUNCH," Renee's mother said, wiping her mouth delicately with her napkin, then setting it on the table in front of her. "I had no idea you were such an accomplished cook, Arlan."

Tate resisted the urge to roll his eyes at his father's smug expression. "He does have good taste." Tate shot an admonishing glance toward his father, who sat at the head of the table in the dining room.

The table was spread with the leftovers of a variety of salads, premade ham and chicken croissants, chicken skewers, crab cakes and artichoke dip. All very delicious and all put together by Kerry at Mug Shots yesterday and delivered last night when Tate was at Renee's.

Tate looked across the table to her, but she was focusing on the croissant she was eating. He was glad he had managed to keep his wits about him during lunch. It had been an awkward affair and, as Addison had said, a complete surprise to him.

Yesterday, holding Renee in his arms had put a crack in his defenses. For the first time since Molly had died, he had held another woman close.

But Renee's life was heading in a direction she wasn't veering from. He would do well to learn from her. When he'd come to Rockyview, his aim was to give his daughter a home and security. To give her his attention. To avoid making the same mistakes he'd made with Molly.

Now he wasn't at all sure where loneliness ended and attraction began. He had to be careful not to risk his heart again.

"I wanted to do something special for both of you," his father was saying to Renee and Brenda. Then his expression softened, and he looked toward Renee, a melancholy look in his eyes. "And in honor of Mother's Day, I especially wanted to do something for you, Renee."

Renee's head shot up at that, her horror-filled eyes shooting toward Addison, then to Arlan.

Tate's heart sank. What was his father thinking? Was he going to reveal the truth about Addison and Renee?

He was about to say something, but Arlan carried on, seemingly oblivious to the heightened tension.

"I see what an attentive daughter you are to your mother," his father was saying. "I wanted to honor that by giving you a break from cooking."

"Hear, hear," Mrs. Albertson said, raising her glass of lemonade. "I propose a toast. To the best daughter a mother could ask for."

Tate quickly relaxed, and saw Renee do the same. Then he quickly raised his own glass, as well. "To a loving and devoted daughter," he said quietly.

A flush worked its way up her neck, and she ducked her head. In spite of his commitment to keep his heart free, he couldn't prevent his reaction to her vulnerability. Her devotion to her mother, her willingness to sacrifice everything for her, was beyond admirable.

"And now, if you'll excuse us," Arlan said, getting up from the table, "Brenda and I are going for a walk around the neighborhood."

"Can I come?" Addison asked, jumping to her feet. "I can push Mrs. Albertson's wheelchair. I'll be really careful."

"Of course you can," Renee's mother said, holding her hand out to Addison. "But you don't need to push the wheelchair unless my arms get tired."

Then Addison looked at the table behind her. "Who is going to clean up?"

"I can."

Tate and Renee spoke at the same time.

"Good. That's settled, then." Arlan rubbed his hands as if everything was going according to plan, and again Tate wondered what his father was up to.

"When will you be back?" Renee asked, laying her napkin down and pushing away from the table.

"I'm sure there's no rush," Mrs. Albertson said, looking over at Renee with a smile that created a twist of apprehension in Tate's stomach. How long was he going to be alone with Renee?

"Do you need help getting the chair out of the house?" Renee asked, making a move to follow them.

"We'll be okay," Arlan said.

Then, with a self-satisfied grin, his father followed Mrs. Albertson out of the room.

Renee watched them leave, her head craned as the front door shut behind them.

Tate heard the muffled rumble of the wheelchair on the metal ramps they had borrowed from a neighbor, then Renee returned, her hands twisted together as she looked over the remnants of lunch.

"You go relax in the living room," Tate said, holding up his hand to forestall the protest he saw forming on Renee's face. "It's Mother's Day. You aren't doing the dishes."

"I don't mind helping. What else would I do?"

Tate wasn't exactly sure he wanted to be so close to Renee for that long, but she was already busy gathering up the leftover food. He stacked up the dirty plates and followed her into the kitchen.

"The food was really good," she said as she set the platter of leftover chicken skewers and artichoke dip onto the tiny kitchen counter.

"I'm sure as a longtime resident of Rockyview you recognized Kerry's menu items," Tate said with a wry note in his voice as he pulled open the dishwasher.

"Mom often orders the dip when we go to Mug Shots." Renee gave him a quick smile, and for a moment the tension permeating the meal dissipated.

Renee pushed up the sleeves of her brown blazer and turned on the faucet to rinse the dishes while Tate took care of the leftovers. She turned to Tate, her expression suddenly serious.

His heart jumping in his chest, his mind slipped back to the kiss they had shared yesterday.

Don't go there, he reminded himself.

"So, I hate to sound old-fashioned, but what are your father's intentions?"

Tate blinked, trying to wrap his head around this sudden shift in their conversation as he dumped the leftover dip into a plastic container. "What?"

"I just need to know what's happening," Renee said, a flush creeping up her neck as she ran the dirty plates under the water. "We are supposed to leave in a couple of months for the therapy program in Vancouver, and...I don't want my mom distracted by...other things."

"Other things meaning my father?" Tate asked.

Renee nodded, and Tate finally realized what she was implying. "You think my dad has a thing for your mom?" he asked, leaning back against the counter, his arms folded over his chest.

Renee carefully set the plates in the open dishwasher as she shrugged. "What else could it be? I mean, first it was the lunch at Mug Shots. Now this. I've caught him looking at her a couple times and not like a friend."

Tate scratched his temple with his index finger, feeling suddenly awkward, then figured he may as well stop dithering. "Actually, I thought he was trying to get us together."

Renee's hands paused, her flush deepening on her face, but she kept her attention on what she was doing.

"He's told me plenty of times what a wonderful person you are." As soon as the words left his mouth, Tate wished he could pull them back, especially after she had made it perfectly clear that she was leaving Rockyview soon.

"Your father has a convenient memory," she muttered.

He wondered what she meant by that.

"At any rate, I think my father is trying to play matchmaker," Tate said. "For us."

Renee looked at him, and when their eyes met, it was as if an electrical current hummed between them.

Yesterday she had shown a side of herself that, he suspected, no one else had ever seen. A bond between them had been created that couldn't be easily ignored or swept aside.

"And here I thought he was making a move on my mother," Renee said, her voice breathless. She laughed, and Tate felt the awareness between them as real as a touch.

"For all I know, he might be doing that, too," Tate said. "Like any lawyer worth his salary, he does know how to multitask."

"I hope not," Renee said quietly.

"I understand your objections given your other plans, but at the same time I'm glad you and your mother came over today," Tate said quietly. "It's good to spend more time with you."

Renee exhaled. "About yesterday—"

Tate stopped her by holding up his hand. "I don't think we need to talk about yesterday." He didn't want to hear her regrets or analyze the reasons he shouldn't have done what he did.

Then her lips shifted into a smile, igniting the faint spark glowing in his soul.

"It's complicated," was all she could say.

Tate knew that. The counselor he'd been seeing with Addison after Molly's death had warned him against bringing women into Addison's life who he wasn't serious about.

Not that Tate had any desire to date anyone after his miserable marriage. But now it seemed he was on the verge of falling for his daughter's natural mother.

When she looked up at him, he saw a yearning in her eyes that called to the loneliness in his own soul. Ignoring the warning bells pealing in his head, he moved closer, caught her head with his hand and brushed a kiss, first over her forehead, then she shifted and their lips met, held.

They both pulled away at the same time. "I don't think... I'm not sure..." She paused, one hand resting on her chest, as if holding on to her heart.

"I'm not, either," he countered.

"This is so complicated," she said quietly, her fingers lightly touching the material of his shirt. "Confusing and yet—"

"It feels right, doesn't it?"

"But Addison is part of this all," she said. "I can't forget about her and neither should you."

"It's because I'm not forgetting about her that I'm thinking this way." He struggled a moment with his reactions to Renee and the tangle of his emotions. But one thing slowly became clear. "I know how this all looks. But Addison is my daughter and your daughter. Why shouldn't we be together?"

"It seems too perfect," she agreed.

"So this brings us back to where we started. What do we do?"

Renee bit her lip as if thinking. Then she pulled back.

"Wait and see, I think."

Tate wasn't sure how to respond to her ambiguous comment. Then Renee spoke again.

"I better go see how my mother is doing," she said, her voice quiet, determined.

But Tate noticed her hands were trembling as she dried them on a towel, then pushed the sleeves of her blazer down. Without another glance his way, she left.

Tate leaned on the counter. He had been so careful. He had guarded his heart not only this past year, but the last few years of his and Molly's marriage, when their relationship had started falling apart. When every interaction with her would end in frustration and anger.

The past few weeks had been amazing, spending time with a woman who was sensitive, caring, kind and a Christian.

All the things he thought he had found in Molly.

Did he dare try again? Did he dare put his and Addison's happiness on the line?

He wished he knew for sure what he was supposed to do. Because whatever he did would have repercussions not only for Addison, but his own wounded and lonely heart.

CHAPTER NINE

"*R*enee. Are you busy?"

Renee looked up from the clipboard she was scribbling on just as her mother wheeled herself around the corner of the shelving unit.

"Not super busy. Just getting some inventory lists together for Cathy. If and when we can ever get this store sold." Renee flipped through the packages of stickers hanging on a hook, counting them as she went, then wrote the amount on the paper attached to the clipboard. She was forging on as if everything was going through. Too much had been happening the past month, and the only way she could keep her balance was to keep her eye on the goal she and her mother had been working toward for the past four years.

"Can we go to the back of the store? I want some privacy."

"Sounds serious." Renee stood aside as her mother wheeled herself down the aisle.

Her mother didn't say anything, and Renee ignored the tinkle of the electronic bell announcing that another customer was coming into the store. Most customers liked to browse before they needed help. She had some time.

They went into the room, and Renee felt a tiny pang of nostalgia. Addison had finished her scrapbook. No more visits from the little girl.

Or her father.

The thought created the usual stew of emotions. Regret and anticipation. Worry and hope. Affection...

She caught herself right there as she carefully closed the door of the back room. Her mother had spun her wheelchair around and was leaning forward, her elbows resting on the arms.

Her mom's cheeks were flushed. Her expression animated. Her eyes bright, enhanced by the pink shirt she had chosen to wear this morning. Brenda usually preferred practical brown or gray. Colors that wouldn't get dirty.

"I want to talk to you about the therapy program," Brenda began. "I was doing some more research about it."

"That's good," Renee said, sitting down on a chair across from her so they were at eye level. "It's good to be informed."

"A little too informed," her mom said, taking Renee's hand and holding it between her own. "I'm concerned about the time commitment. It might take more than a year, and that's only if everything goes well."

"We talked about that," Renee said, squeezing her mother's hand. "The therapy team told us that you are a good candidate."

Brenda nodded slowly, as if absorbing this information. "Yes. But I've been in this wheelchair for eight years. And I know that every year I've spent here means my muscles have atrophied that much more, in spite of the exercises we've been doing."

"That's why they warned us that it would take a year to a year and a half." Three weeks ago it would have simply been twelve to sixteen months she would carve out of her life for her mother.

But now?

Images of Tate slid through her mind.

Did she dare hope that something important was beginning between them?

And what about Addison? Renee had already missed so much of her life—could she really walk away from her so easily?

Her mother sighed gently. "What would you say if I told you I don't want to leave Rockyview? That I don't want to enroll in the program?"

It took a few moments for Brenda's words to sink in.

"What? Why wouldn't you want to do this?" Renee asked. "It'll get you out of your wheelchair. You'll be able to walk again."

"Maybe, and maybe not. Even if I could walk again, there's no guarantee I won't need a walker to help me. I'll still have limited mobility."

Renee fought the reservations that always rose up when reality and her dreams for her mother collided. "The therapist gave us decent odds. About sixty to seventy percent mobility."

"With a thirty to forty percent chance that nothing will change," her mother continued. "I think the cost is too great for the return."

Renee knew the odds. Those thoughts had circulated ever since they'd visited the clinic six months ago. "But the therapy is noninvasive, and what do you have to lose if it works?"

"Over a year of our lives and giving up everything we've built up here on a chance. A possibility." Her mother leaned forward, her eyes bright. "I know it's a dream of yours, and, for a while, it was a dream of mine. But I also know how many dreams this store and the business has fulfilled for you."

This store had been a uniting factor for the two of them. They had spent many therapeutic hours planning, buying inventory, starting up classes, expanding the business into custom printing and design. That the store did so well spoke to how well they worked together.

"I've always had a bigger dream, Mom. To see you walk

again."

"I know that. But my dreams have changed recently."

Renee felt an agitated undertow of resistance at what she was saying. But beneath all that, she felt the faintest drift of...relief?

If Brenda didn't want to leave Rockyview, they could stay. Their life would go on.

Could something really happen now between her and Tate? If she and her mother didn't leave town for the therapy program, they would have time to explore the growing feelings between them.

But how could she condone such a drastic change in their plans? Plans she had made for her mother's own good.

"What's changed?" Renee asked, confusion battling with the myriad other emotions she was experiencing.

Brenda blushed, then looked down. "I can't tell you right now. It's too soon."

"Too soon for what? Can you be any more vague?"

"Don't be flip. I just can't tell you right now."

"Mom, you're talking about putting off something we've discussed repeatedly. Plans we've made for the past three, four years."

"I know, but I feel as though I'm seeing things more clearly. We both know this store isn't selling, and it's causing pressure for you. We might not meet the deadline."

"We can borrow the money."

Her mother gave her a patient look. "We've looked into that option, and you know it's not going to happen. So, speak to the chief therapist. Ask him if they can put the program off for a couple of months. Even a year."

"A year? You know how long it took us to get into this program? There might not be a space coming up for a couple of years again."

"Then I'll call them. Tell them I'm dropping out."

Renee recognized the look in her mother's eyes. It was the same one Renee got when she wanted to do something and her mother wouldn't let her.

"Can you give me a good reason for this sudden change of heart? Something more than 'it's too soon'?"

Her mother held up her hand in a stop gesture. "Call the doctor and tell him to postpone it."

Her mother's comments reinforced the doubts Renee had stifled ever since their initial visit to the specialist who had spoken to them about the therapy. But she had spent so much time and energy on this, she didn't feel she could give up without a fight.

"We'll be having a conference call with the chief therapist and his assistants next Thursday, and I'll bring it up then. Before I do that, however, I want you to really think about this and pray about it, and I'll do the same. We'll talk again in a few days."

"What do you think I've been doing already?" Renee accepted the faint reprimand with a slight inclination of her head.

"I'm sure you have been, Mom," Renee said, reaching over to take her mother's hand between hers and squeeze it. "You know this program has repercussions for me, as well."

"And a lot of obligation." Her mother reached over with her other hand and stroked Renee's hair away from her face. "You are an amazing daughter, Renee. I thank the Lord every day for you," she said quietly. Then she wheeled herself backward, spun around, opened the door and headed out of the room.

Renee watched her go. She closed her eyes and, as she always did, asked God to forgive her. Then she drew in a deep breath, knowing that, in the next couple of days, she had a lot of praying to do.

But even as she prayed, glimmers of hope flickered in her soul at the repercussions of not leaving Rockyview.

Was it now possible to think about her and Tate? She knew

she hadn't imagined the shift in their relationship. Her feelings for him grew every time they were together, and she sensed he felt the same. Could she truly explore the possibilities of that now?

She pushed the questions aside and got back to work. For now, she had to act as if nothing had changed. Tonight she was going to call Freddy. No matter what happened in the next month, she still wanted that lien resolved and off the store.

❦

Two hours and one quick sandwich later, Renee closed up the store, locking the door behind her, relishing being outside for the first time since noon.

She slipped her book bag over her shoulder and was about to cross the street to Evangeline's store, Shelf Awareness, when she heard someone call her name. Her heart skipped a beat when she recognized Tate's voice.

She hadn't seen or heard from him since Mother's Day. She knew things were changing between them, but she hardly dared look too far into the future. Once, it seemed so clear. However, in the past couple of weeks, it had grown less distinct.

"Renee, wait up."

She saw Tate striding toward her, briefcase in one hand, blazer bunched in the other. His chin was shadowed by stubble and his hair, usually immaculately groomed, was disheveled. His white button-down shirt, which he had rolled up the sleeves of, was tucked into faded blue jeans that he wore with cowboy boots.

Her heart did a flip-flop as he came nearer, his casually scruffy look giving him an appealing vulnerability.

"Hey there," she said, her voice just a little shakier than usual.

"Hey, yourself. You done for the day?"

She nodded, clasping her book bag with both hands as if she

120

needed something solid to cling to. She poked her thumb over her shoulder at Evangeline's bookstore. "Just heading over to my book club."

"What book are you reading?"

"A mystery that takes place in Nigeria. It was Mia's choice. She tends to like detective novels and murder mysteries. She has two boys and twin girls, and she's on her own. Why she'd want to read about murder and mayhem on her time off surprises me." Renee stopped talking, realizing that her nervousness around Tate was making her babble.

"What books do you enjoy?" Tate's smile lit a spark of wonder.

"I've been accused of liking dark and depressing books. Maybe it's indicative of my personality," she said with a self-deprecating smile.

"I wouldn't say that," Tate returned, tossing his dark blazer over his shoulder and hooking it with his index finger. He gave her a crooked grin that didn't help her equilibrium one iota. "Anyone who works in a store so full of glitter and ribbon and color can't possibly have a dark personality."

Renee noted the slight fan of wrinkles at the corners of his eyes and the way the sun glinted off his hair.

"I actually have a reason for accosting you on the street like this," Tate said, his gaze keeping hers captive. "Tanner Bond invited me to take my horses out on the trails behind his ranch. Thought it would be a good way to give the horses some exercise." He shrugged. "You said you used to ride, so I thought you might enjoy coming along."

The invitation was a surprise.

"I'm not much of a rider," she said. "Like I told you, not so much riding as hanging on. And a lot of laughing."

"I'm not doing the steeplechase," Tate retorted.

Renee paused, thinking of the possibilities. She'd be spending another afternoon with Tate.

"I thought you might enjoy the ride," he continued.

"Don't you have to work?"

"I'm taking the afternoon off. With my father's blessing. Besides, I don't have such a heavy caseload yet. Still new in town, I guess." He added a grin that sent her foolish heart into overdrive. "I know that Wednesdays you often have Ashley coming in to help you, so I figured it would be okay to ask."

She couldn't suppress her smile at the thought of spending time with Tate. Alone.

"She does, so it would work out." She was done with inventory and didn't have much else going on. She was fairly sure her mother wouldn't mind. "Will Addison be coming, as well?"

Tate shook his head. "No, she'll be in school. I'll pick you up at noon, if that's okay?" Then he pursed his lips. "I forgot—will you need someone to watch your mother?"

"Ashley is coming, as you said, and I do believe there's cell phone reception up that mountain."

"Right. Sure. Then we've both got everything covered." Tate rocked back on his cowboy boots, then flashed Renee another smile that made her heart skip a beat. "I'll see you tomorrow, then." He took a step closer then, as if it was the most normal thing in the world, dropped a light kiss on her mouth.

Renee leaned into him, then when he drew back, felt the cool air on her heated cheeks.

"Okay. See you then," she said, breathless, then turned and stepped out into the street, narrowly missing a collision with a young boy on a bicycle.

"Hey, watch it, lady," the boy called out as Renee hurriedly glanced left, then right, then behind her to where Tate was still watching her.

"You okay?" he called out as she made it to the other side.

She waved off his concern, then stepped into Evangeline's bookstore, feeling like a flustered teenager. She was acting like an idiot. Why couldn't she be all calm and collected?

Because it had been years since she had allowed any man into her life, past the barriers she'd erected almost nine years ago.

Evangeline was bagging up the purchases of a man who looked to be in his mid-thirties, sandy-brown hair, pleasant features. He didn't look familiar, but he was having an animated discussion with her.

Renee worked her way around the other side of the colorful display of children's books, interspersed with stuffed animals and building blocks, so she wouldn't look as if she was eaves-dropping.

The walls of the store were lined with fiction on one side, nonfiction on the other, and between them there were chest-high shelves holding craft books, recipe books, picture books and children's books.

Renee paused at the young children's section. Maybe Addison would like a book, she thought, pulling out a chapter book that was part of a series dealing with girls and horses.

As she opened the book, Renee allowed her mind to wander. Her and Tate and Addison.

Her daughter.

Renee clutched the book against her chest, afraid to allow her hope to fully take root, yet realizing that she and Tate were moving toward something more serious.

Dear Lord, she prayed. *I hardly dare hope. Hardly dare dream. Please help me to trust that You will take me through this all. Help me to know You will watch out for me.*

"You okay?"

Renee's head shot up at her friend's question. She looked around, as if getting her bearings.

"Yeah. I'm fine."

"And I'm finally done for the day. I thought Jeff would never leave."

"Jeff?"

"Deptuck. He's the new fireman in town. He's been assigned to do a potential-hazard assessment on the stores downtown, especially this bookstore and Mia's flower shop. Plus, he heard about our book club and wants to join." Evangeline rolled her eyes. "I think he's just trying to find a way to make a move on Angie."

"You sound jealous."

Evangeline waved her comment off.

"What's the problem? He's cute and single," Renee continued with a grin.

"Not my type."

"Why? Because he doesn't talk with an English accent? Not too many dukes and lords around Rockyview, my girl."

"No, but Tate is here," Evangeline said. "Kissing you in broad daylight. Looks like things are getting pretty serious between you two."

Renee smiled slightly. She wasn't sure she wanted the tentative emotions she and Tate were dealing with brought out into the bright light of day.

But at the same time, having Evangeline to talk to about it helped make it seem more real.

"We're taking it one step at a time," Renee said quietly.

"Of course. I imagine he's considering Addison's needs," Evangeline said. "Are you thinking of buying that?"

Renee looked down at the book she was holding and smiled. "I thought I would give it to Addison."

"I know she likes horses, just like her dad."

"She does. In fact, we are... Tate is taking me riding tomorrow afternoon. At Tanner Bond's ranch."

"Nice." Evangeline's expression turned all starry-eyed. "Horseback riding with Tate and no kids. How romantic."

"What's romantic?" Mia Verbeek called out, coming out of the back room of the bookstore, pulling her sweater off and tossing it into a chair Evangeline had set out in a corner. "I hope you're not talking about the book yet. We're the only ones here right now."

"No. I'm talking about the ride Renee is taking with Tate tomorrow. And I'm talking about the kiss Tate popped on Miss Albertson's innocent lips just a few moments ago."

Mia's eyes widened, and her mouth fell open. "Really? Tate and our Renee?"

"It was just a kiss," Renee said, trying to bring everything back into perspective. If she didn't dial things down, her friends would have her married off by the end of the evening.

Mia waggled a finger of denial. "Says the woman who only two weeks ago told us she wasn't pining for any man, especially not Tate Truscott." She gave Evangeline a smug look.

Once again Renee felt a flush warming her cheeks. Seriously, she was reverting to high school.

"And the blush tells it all," Mia said with a victorious grin.

Renee took a breath, then held her hand up. "Please, girls, you have to keep this quiet. Tate has Addison to think of, and it's not fair if, well, if she thinks something is happening and it isn't."

"Then Tate shouldn't have kissed you on Main Street."

They all laughed, but then Evangeline patted Renee on the shoulder, her expression growing more serious. "We'll keep it quiet. I promise." Then she shook her head, her expression growing dreamy again. "This is so great."

"Yeah. Maybe you might even have something positive to say about the romance novel Evangeline picked," Mia added, giving Renee a gentle elbow in the side as they walked to the back of the store.

"I just might," Renee returned. "Though I have to admit, it was better than some of the other ones you've picked," she said to Evangeline.

"Perspective," her friend said, sweeping her hair back from her face. "It's all a matter of perspective."

CHAPTER TEN

"*H*old easy there, Bandit." Tate caught the restive horse's bridle and held it just long enough to catch his attention. The bay settled and flicked his ears, looking back as if to apologize.

Tate patted him on the neck, then went back to adjusting the stirrups for Renee.

He glanced over his shoulder to where Renee stood, chatting with Sabine and Tanner. Her blue jeans looked good on her, as did the gray corduroy shirt and puffy green vest. She wore her hair loose, and a stray breeze tossed it around her face in a halo of golden-brown.

Renee pushed her hair back with her hand, then she shot him a smiling glance over her shoulder. As always, Tate felt the curious connection between them. More and more, he realized each moment he spent with her cemented his feelings for her.

Sabine walked over and he looked up.

"You got Renee's stirrups adjusted?" Sabine asked.

"All ready to go," he said, giving one final tug, just to make sure. Bandit stamped and snorted as Tate's horse moved closer to him.

"So you know where to go?" Sabine asked, shifting her baby on her arm and patting Duke, Tate's palomino.

"Tanner gave me directions, and I have my cell phone in case I get really lost," Tate said with a grin.

Sabine glanced over to Renee, who was talking to Tanner. "I don't think getting lost with Renee would be such a bad thing," she said.

Tate looked over at Renee, who was laughing at something Tanner said.

Then Renee walked toward him, a vague smile edging her lips.

"Hey. Got your horse ready to go," he said. "Do you need a hand getting up?"

"I'm okay," she said. Then with one surprisingly agile move she mounted up, settled in the saddle and shook her hair back from her face as she caught up the reins. Bandit shuffled his hooves, snorted again and shook his head, but Renee didn't seem fazed by his behavior.

"He's a good horse," Tate told her, handing up the halter rope to her. "Just eager to get going."

"We'll get along just fine, won't we, boy?" Renee said, giving Bandit a couple of pats on the neck. As she straightened, she gave Tate a wide smile. "I'm looking forward to this. I haven't been riding in so long."

"You look pretty natural," he said, looking up at her, silhouetted against a blue sky edged by the mountains beyond.

She shrugged off his praise, but her smile told him that she took it to heart.

"Just so you know, if you get up to the pasture, there's a fork in the trail that will bring you past an old trapper's cabin," Sabine said to Renee. "But if you keep going along the pasture, you'll find a spot where you get a gorgeous view of the valley. Just keep the Shadow Woman's mountain on your right and you won't get lost."

"Thanks for the tip," Renee said. "And thanks again for letting us ride here."

"No problem. If you two aren't back by dark, though, we'll send a search party."

Renee laughed again.

Tate climbed onto the saddle of his horse. He settled in, then turned to Renee. "Ready?"

"You have the snacks?" Sabine asked.

Tate leaned over to check the saddlebag that Sabine had packed for them, and nodded.

"Have fun," Sabine said, stepping back as she lifted Courtney to her shoulder, patting the little bundle of baby. Her tiny head wavered a moment, then dropped onto Sabine's shoulder.

Tate caught Renee watching them, a rueful expression on her face.

Was she thinking of the day she'd given Addison away?

"Have a good time," Sabine called out as she walked back to the house, still holding her baby close.

Tate waved, then pulled his horse around, following a well-worn trail leading away from the ranch.

They rode past the corrals, then a small cabin, then down a well-worn path toward the hills tucked against the mountains.

He looked back to check on Renee, only to catch her looking at him, her smile lighting up her features.

"Don't get us lost," she said with a laugh.

"I'll try not to," he returned.

They crossed a wooden bridge, the hooves of the horses beating out a hollow, uneven rhythm, the water bubbling over rocks beneath them.

They hit the path beyond, and then the trail wound into the tall, shadowy trees. The utter silence of the forest, broken only by the footfalls of the horses on the damp ground, washed over Tate, easing away the busyness of the week. The path was wide enough that he and Renee could ride side by side.

"I'm so glad you invited me along," Renee said. "It's so wonderful to be riding again."

"I'm glad you came, too," he said, looking at her, then at the trail ahead of them, dappled by the sunshine breaking through the canopy of leaves that sheltered them. "This is amazing."

Renee looked away from him, leaning to one side as if trying to see something.

"Are you looking for something?"

"I think it's too early, but from up here you can often see the Shadow Woman that Sabine was talking about."

"Shadow Woman? What is that?"

"It's a legend. Not sure of the origin. But it's about a woman who was done wrong by her man and is waiting for him to return. She only shows up like a shadow picture on the mountain when the light is just right."

"Where is she?"

Renee stopped her horse and pointed. "See that rock face? The sheer bluff above the trees to the right of that huge cleft? The shadow is on that rock face. You can just see her coming out. She's wearing a dress, looking like she's leaning forward, as if she's waiting."

"Did her love ever come back for her?" Tate asked, resting his arms on the horn of his saddle as he squinted at the rock face.

"He did, but not right away."

"That's good. I prefer the endings of my story to be happy," he said, turning to look at her.

She shrugged then looked away. "That doesn't always happen."

He wondered if she was referring to her own story, but decided to leave it be.

"When you and Addison went riding, back in Ontario, where would you go?" Renee asked.

"There were parks with riding paths, but they were nothing

like this." Tate looked behind him at the creek that ran down the hill beside them.

"Will the horses be okay?"

"They're a bit out of shape, but we won't be riding them hard today. Tanner said it was an easy trail."

They rode in silence for a while, climbing higher with every step. Tate's attention was divided between working with his horse and the welcome distraction of Renee beside him.

He shot another glance her way, then moved his horse closer. "You were okay with leaving your shop for the afternoon?"

"To go riding?" Renee motioned to the break in the trees. "Oh, yeah."

They already looked down on the pastures of Tanner's ranch. Beyond the fields rose the mountains, skirted with green breaking to rugged rocks, the jagged peaks iced with glistening snow.

"Pretty incredible," Tate said. "I'm so glad I made the decision to move here. I can't imagine that this will be available to me anytime I want."

"It is spectacular. I'll miss it if—" Renee stopped speaking, and Tate knew she was talking about when she and her mother would leave.

He felt a twist of sorrow and a whispering of second thoughts, but latched onto the last word she ended the sentence with. "What do you mean, 'if'?"

Renee sighed. "I'm not sure if we're going anymore. My mother's been talking about postponing the program, even dropping out of it altogether."

"Is she sure about that?" Tate asked, his optimism rising. Renee might not be leaving.

"She's sure enough. I can't make her do this, and if she's not one hundred percent committed to the therapy, it won't work."

"Why do you think she's changed her mind?"

Renee shrugged. "She was talking about the success rate, which isn't a hundred percent, but she's known that from the beginning. My mother doesn't let go of an idea easily. So whatever is making her change her mind, I think it's pretty big."

Then another thought washed over Tate like a bucket of ice water. "Could she have found out...about Addison?"

Renee gave a decisive shake of her head. "She doesn't know. Not from me. I was afraid that if she did find out, she'd postpone the therapy for sure. But I've been careful, and I imagine you and your father have, as well. Besides, it isn't only my secret to keep."

Tate nodded, his saddle creaking as he moved. "My father is a principled man. Client confidentiality is sacrosanct with him."

"So Addison isn't the reason, as far as I know," Renee said, tugging slightly on the reins, holding her horse back to keep pace with Tate's. "But, as I said, she's adamant."

Tate was unable to stop an uplifting rush of happiness. If the program was postponed, maybe even put off, Renee would be free to make plans. For the future.

Did he dare take a chance? In spite of what Renee just told him, he couldn't help but feel cautious, concerned.

"And how do you feel about her decision?" Tate asked.

Renee looked ahead, frowning as she contemplated his question.

"I'm not so sure how I feel anymore. Once, it was the most important thing in my life. I thought her healing would...free me."

Tate heard the hitch in her voice and nudged his horse lightly in the ribs, a signal to move sideways. Closer to Renee's horse. "Free you from guilt?" He spoke the words quietly. Simply.

Renee nodded. "And though I've tried to let go, I still feel guilty about my mother being in the wheelchair."

"It was an accident," Tate said, keeping his voice low,

nonthreatening. "A mistake made by a young girl who had a lot to deal with."

Renee looked away, out over the vista they caught from time to time through the trees.

The creek was like a silver ribbon unspooling across the fields. The buildings of the ranch lay below them like tiny boxes dotting the yard. Tate hadn't realized how far they had climbed.

"I've told myself that, and though my mother has forgiven me repeatedly," Renee said, her voice a hushed sound barely audible above the breeze whispering through the trees above, "it's hard to let go when I'm faced with the consequences of what I've done every time I look at my mother in the wheelchair. Kind of hard to know what to do with all that guilt."

"And you think it would go away if your mother could walk again?"

"I always thought if she got better, then all the sacrifices I made would be worth it."

"The sacrifice of giving up Addison."

"Yes."

Tate was quiet, uncertain how to deal with this revelation. He couldn't treat it lightly. Yet, when she had broken down in his arms, she had confessed to feelings she hadn't shared with too many others. It had created a bond between them that he couldn't deny.

Please, Lord, help me to say the right thing. Help her to feel Your forgiveness. To know she is carrying burdens she doesn't need to carry.

"Do you think God has forgiven you?" he asked.

Renee's head spun around so quickly her horse startled. She reached down and patted Bandit on the neck, speaking soothing words. Then she sat up again, tossing him a puzzled look. "Why do you ask that?"

"I'm thinking you keep picking up a burden of guilt that your mother and God have tried repeatedly to take away from you."

"Forgiveness doesn't change the repercussions of the accident both for my mother and Addison." Renee's voice carried a harsh note, as if she was trying to convince herself more than Tate.

"If your mother has forgiven you, I would be sure God has even more so."

Renee said nothing for a while, and Tate hoped he hadn't overstepped a line.

"Maybe." She conveyed a stark look. "Seems too easy to just let go, though."

"Always does," Tate said. "I think you need to set aside what you think should happen. You need to trust that your mother has prayed about this, as well. Maybe you need to know that God is not only in charge of your mother's life, but yours, as well."

Renee shook her head, her hair falling across her cheek. She pushed it aside, then looked at him. "I think if I were completely honest, part of me is relieved that my mother doesn't want to go through with the therapy. That's also what I've been struggling with."

"But why?"

"I was worried myself about the program. What if it didn't help Mom as I'd hoped? What if, after all that time and money, nothing changed? And, the reality is, there are other things to consider now." She looked directly at him, a smile on her lips. "I have other things on my mind confusing me and shifting my priorities." She laughed.

"And that would be?" he prompted, sensing she needed help articulating what they might be.

"You."

That single word found a sweet place in his heart, soothing away his misgivings. This was okay. This could work.

Right?

He pushed aside his concerns. Right now he was up in the

beautiful mountains, alone with a woman who was growing more important to him by the day.

He reached over and took her hand in his.

"You've been on my mind, as well."

Renee caught her lip between her teeth, her hand tightening her grip on his, her face silhouetted against the green of the trees behind her. "We said we'd go along and see where this led." Her eyes shone with a light that kindled his hope. "And I like where it's leading."

"You're allowed to be happy, Renee," Tate said, trying to sound neutral.

Renee's smile blossomed. "It just seems too good to be true."

Then she leaned over, and her lips brushed his cheek. The horses pulled away from each other, and Renee laughed. Tate reined his horse in, and Renee did the same.

Then he leaned closer, and this time they shared a proper kiss. When they broke away, he smiled at her, and lifted her hand to his lips.

For now, nothing more needed to be said.

He suppressed all his worries and concerns about Addison. Right now, he was spending time with the woman who had captured his heart.

The mother of his daughter.

⚜

"THAT'S a lovely color on you. You haven't worn that dress in ages."

Renee looked down at the dress she had spent half an hour trying to pick out. A soft peach wrap dress that Renee had updated with a wide, brown belt and a shrug. She didn't usually dress up this much for church. She'd had no reason to before.

Before Tate.

"I also love how you're wearing your hair," her mother

added.

Renee looked away from her mother's knowing eyes. "I thought I would try something different." She had pulled her hair off to one side and secured it with a pearl comb, allowing the rest of her hair to spill over her shoulder in a cascade of curls.

Renee swiped lipstick over her lips, trying not to criticize herself and the faults she always found in her features—nose too long and thin, eyes too wide apart, forehead too high.

"You managed to get all dressed up, too," Renee said, noticing for the first time her mother's skirt and blazer. The aqua shirt she wore had an attached silk scarf her mom had tied in a bow. The drop pearl earrings Renee's father had given her on their twentieth anniversary glinted from her ears. Renee hadn't seen her mother wear the earrings or the suit since her father's death. "Special occasion?"

Brenda gave her a demure smile. "I might ask you the same question."

Renee returned her smile, thankful to see her so happy. In fact, Renee hadn't seen her this carefree in years.

She wanted to ask her why, but something held her back. She was still deciding whether to push her mother about the therapy program or leave it be.

Renee parked in their usual spot close to the church, and as she stepped out of the van, she saw Tate's father striding toward them, his grin making her wonder what was going on.

But soon she realized he wasn't looking at her.

He was looking directly at her mother.

"Good morning, Brenda," he said as the lift holding the wheelchair whirred to the ground. "What a treat to see you looking so well."

"Thank you, Arlan." Her mother's hand fluttered up to touch her hair.

Arlan Truscott brushed her shoulder with his hand, then

stood aside as her mother maneuvered the wheelchair off the van lift.

"Can I walk with you?" he asked.

"That would be lovely."

Brenda folded her hands in her lap as Arlan grabbed the handles of the wheelchair. He then shot Renee a quick glance. "I'm sorry—do you mind?"

It seemed strange to let someone else take over, but she knew it would be ungracious to refuse him.

"No. Not at all," Renee said as she hit the button to move the lift back into the van. She watched them go, snippets of their conversation drifting back to her, fragments of laughter. Renee suddenly realized she hadn't heard her mother's carefree laugh in a long, long time.

She closed the door of the van, got her purse, then hurried to catch up. By the time she stepped into the foyer, Arlan was already wheeling her mother to the elevator.

"Renee. There you are!"

Addison's exuberant voice behind her created a frisson of yearning and delight. She turned, and when she saw Tate standing beside Addison, her heart did a slow backflip.

"I was looking for you," Addison said, swinging her father's hand. "Where's your mom?"

Tate gave Addison an affectionate smile, then looked back to Renee. "I'm guessing my father absconded with your mother, leaving you all alone."

"That means you have to sit with us." Addison caught Renee's hand in hers, and Renee looked from Tate to Addison with eyes glowing with pleasure.

"Renee might want to sit with her mother," Tate warned.

"Nope. She has to sit with us. Please, Daddy," Addison pleaded.

Renee looked down at Addison, clinging to the little girl's hand as love swept over her in a tidal wave of emotions. Addison's innocent gesture opened a place in Renee's soul she had kept tightly shut all these years.

Then she looked up at Tate, who was giving her a careful smile, as if unsure of the situation himself.

"I don't mind sitting by myself," she said, giving him an out.

"No. That would be silly, right, Daddy? You come sit with us," Addison insisted.

"I guess it's easier to do what Addison wants," Tate said, giving her a lopsided smile, which only enhanced the feelings filling Renee's heart.

Hope and love washed over her. Beneath them was the reality that she was falling for Tate. That he was becoming intrinsically woven into the fabric of her life.

"Let's go sit down," Addison said, pulling Renee and Tate along with her.

They came to the top of the stairs just as Arlan was pushing Renee's mother down the aisle of the church to her usual spot. He bent over her, as if to make sure everything was okay, then with a wide smile, sat down beside her.

As Renee saw him settle in the pew, then reach over to take her mother's hand, all the events of the past week meshed together. Arlan was the reason her mother didn't want to move to Vancouver anymore.

Renee suddenly realized she might not be all alone caring for her mother anymore. She drew in a long, cleansing breath, then glanced over at Tate, who was also looking at their parents. But a frown furrowed his brow.

"Did you know about this?" she whispered, leaning closer to him, tipping her head toward their parents.

"Not really," he whispered back. "But my dad's been acting kind of strange lately."

"Let's go sit down," Addison ordered, tugging on them again.

Renee and Tate shared another look, then followed their demanding daughter down the aisle.

CHAPTER ELEVEN

"*I* got new shoes," Addison was telling Renee, swinging her legs back and forth in the church pew, admiring the shiny, black Mary Janes adorning her feet. "My daddy bought them for me."

"They are beautiful," Renee said.

Then Addison leaned against Renee.

Tate's heart faltered at the sight. Yes, Renee was Addison's mother, but the situation between them was tentative. He had to be careful.

And yet...

Then Addison elbowed him. "Daddy. Can Renee come to my school play next week?"

Tate looked down at his daughter, feeling as if he was being pulled in two directions. "I think she might be working at the store," he said, giving Addison a careful look.

Addison frowned, then glanced over at Renee, who had the same expectant look on her face.

In that instant he saw Renee in Addison's face. In the curve of her jaw and the set of her eyes. His heart faltered.

Then Renee gave a perfunctory nod. "Of course," she said quietly. "I...I will be busy."

"Can't you get Ashley to help you?" Addison asked, her voice rising in protest.

"Inside voice, please," Renee said, touching Addison lightly on the nose.

"Maybe Renee can come another time," Tate said, slipping his arm around Addison's shoulders.

Addison wrinkled up her face in dismay and looked as if she was about to lodge another protest. Thankfully, the choir started up, and Addison joined in, switching easily from disappointment to exuberance.

Glancing over at Renee, he saw that she pulled her hand out of Addison's and folded hers on her lap. Tate reached across Addison's shoulder and touched Renee's, giving it a light squeeze, reconnecting with her.

She looked at him, and her smile seemed to say, *I understand.*

Which made her all the more appealing to him.

But where did her relationship with him end and her relationship with Addison begin?

Truth be told, he would prefer to keep Addison and Renee in different parts of his life. At least until he was sure of how things were proceeding with Renee.

He forced his attention back to the minister, who was announcing that he would be preaching on a passage from Psalm 52 today. Tate picked up a Bible and, as he always did, gave it to Addison. She found the passage, then held it up so they both could read the words.

"But I am like an olive tree flourishing in the house of God; I trust in God's unfailing love for ever and ever."

Tate repeated the words again, centering himself. He knew that he had to trust in God's unfailing love to guide him through this tangle. And he also knew, in every decision of his life, he had to learn to put God first.

When they were done, he dropped the Bible back into the rack, ready to focus on the minister and not the beautiful woman sitting beside his daughter.

⟨⟨⟩⟩

"So, Mom, you've been running around the store all morning," Renee said, standing in front of her mother's chair to block her way. "We need to talk."

They stood in the ribbon aisle, with Renee located between her mother and the back room.

"What do we need to talk about?" she asked, her mother's voice as innocent as a child's.

"Sunday." Renee dropped her hands on her hips in an I-mean-business gesture. "How we ended up at the Truscotts' again for lunch, and how you've been so busy since Sunday that you haven't had much time for the store?"

Her mother gave her an arch look. "Or we could talk about that little walk you and Tate went on after church."

Renee tried without much success to suppress the blush that raced up her neck.

Arlan and her mother had urged her and Tate to go for a walk after lunch. They wouldn't leave it alone, so she and Tate had gone, Addison staying behind. They hadn't talked much, but once she and Tate were away from the house, they'd managed to steal a few kisses. Since then, he'd been texting her every day, each trill of her phone sending an answering trill in her heart.

Renee hadn't been this happy in years.

However, she needed to discuss important things with her mother.

"Then let's talk about how, when you pushed me and Tate out the door to go for that walk, you and Arlan left with the van and took Addison, and Tate had to drive me home in his vehicle.

Maybe we should talk about what's happening between you and Arlan."

Her mother gave Renee a coquettish smile, then tilted her head to one side. "I'm not sure what you mean."

Renee tried not to get frustrated with her mother. "I'm thinking your matchmaking had more to do with you and Arlan than me and Tate."

Brenda merely smiled, and stayed silent.

"So you and Arlan...?" Renee let the question linger, encouraging her mother to finish it.

Brenda gave her daughter a coy look. "And you and Tate?"

"C'mon, Mom, this isn't junior high. I'll tell if you will."

The store's bell jangled, announcing the arrival of customers, and the moment was about to pass. But she couldn't let it go.

"Then I won't tell." Her mother spun her wheelchair around and headed to the back room. "I've got a card-making class to get ready for. Did you make sure we have enough chartreuse and mauve card stock for the projects? And ribbon. I know we were short of that."

"We have all we need," Renee said as she followed her mother into the room, then shut the door behind them, closing off the outside world for a moment. Her phone buzzed in her pocket and she smiled. Another text from Tate no doubt, but she ignored it as she sat down, putting herself at eye level with her mother.

"Mom, you and I both know we're under a time crunch. Tomorrow we'll be having that conference call with the therapy team, and you'll have to tell them what you want. I need to make sure you're not postponing all this for the wrong reasons."

Brenda folded her arms and tucked in her chin.

Not a good sign, Renee thought. If there was one language she was fluent in, it was her mother's body language.

"I have my reasons for my decisions," her mother said. "I was going to let you know soon. However, I had to make sure the...situation I was involved in was going the way I had hoped, and that I wasn't misreading the circumstances."

"Between you and Arlan," Renee said, reeling her mother back to the point.

"I think he loves me."

"Loves you?"

"And I love him."

"You love him?" Renee parroted what her mother told her. "How...when...?"

"If you must know, it started because of you and Tate. Arlan had been helping me write up my will—"

"Your will?"

"Yes. I like to be prepared. Anyhow, at one of our meetings he told me his son was coming to town. I joked that we should get the two of you together. He thought it was a great idea. So we started planning. And then when Addison talked about making a scrapbook, we both thought that was the perfect solution."

As her mother talked, Renee felt as if all the pieces of a convoluted puzzle slowly fell into place.

Tate had mentioned how his father had encouraged Addison to make the scrapbook. She remembered her mother's approval that Renee be the one to work with Tate and Addison.

"So the meeting at Mug Shots...and the Mother's Day dinner...?" Renee let the sentence drift off in a question.

"All part of the plan. Look how well it worked. You and Tate seem happy together. I know he's been texting you all morning."

"How—"

"Seriously, Renee. You're as transparent as vellum. Your phone rings, you pull it out of your pocket and then you get that look on your face."

"What look?" Renee protested.

"That sappy, lovey-dovey—"

"Mom," Renee protested. "You started telling me about you and Arlan. Let's get back to that."

Her mother shrugged and then it was her turn to get a sappy look on her face. "While we were planning to get the two of you together, there was a...fortunate...side effect."

"You and Arlan fell in love."

Her mother looked down at her hands. "Yes. We care very much for each other. Trust me, honey, it was as much of a surprise to us as it is to you."

Renee released a gentle laugh. "This is an interesting predicament," she said. "I never thought—"

"Me neither. I never thought someone like me could attract a man. But Arlan is loving, kind and generous, and he told me that he loves me just the way I am."

"That's why you don't want to go through with the therapy program in Vancouver?"

Her mother nodded. "I don't want to be so far away from him. We've talked about marriage," Brenda said quietly.

Renee sat back in her chair, still trying to absorb what her mom had just told her, and all the implications for her.

"It's premature, I know," Brenda continued, "but I thought I should let you know what's at stake here."

Myriad emotions swirled through Renee's mind. Hope. Happiness for her mother. Fear of the repercussions of this decision. Fear for what would happen to her mother if Arlan realized the full scope of Brenda's care.

She didn't know how to process all this in a way that made sense to her.

Then her cell phone rang. Like a drowning sailor she pounced on it, glancing at the display. Tate.

"Hey," she said, thankful for the diversion. "How's it going?"

"Can you come to the office?"

"Now?"

"Now would be nice," he said, his deep voice holding a hint of promise. "I need to talk to you."

And she needed to talk to him, too. She realized that she had someone special. Someone other than her mother that she could talk to. Share things with.

"Yeah. That would work just fine."

"See you soon."

Renee couldn't stop smiling as she ended the call, then looked over at her mother, who was smirking at her. "I'm guessing that was Tate," she said.

"You can guess all you want," Renee said, pushing herself to her feet. "But I'll be gone for an hour or so."

"Stay as long as you want."

Renee just shook her head. "We'll talk more tonight," she warned. "And we are still going to take that call on Thursday."

Her mother nodded as Renee stifled a flicker of panic. Pulling out of the therapy program was her mom's decision. And Renee had to trust that this was truly what her mother wanted.

But part of her still felt it was the wrong thing to do. Part of her felt that all wrongs would be made right if she could see her mother free from that chair.

Still felt that she could move on with her life only if everything was right in her mother's world.

CHAPTER TWELVE

Jate clicked his mouse and sent the last email. As he looked at the clock on the wall, he heard voices in the outer office. Debbie's rough laugh, Renee's lilting reply.

As he got to his feet, the door opened and there she was.

The light from the outer office highlighted her hair, putting her in silhouette.

"Come on in," he said, trying not to rush as he walked around his desk to her side.

As she closed the door behind her, he gave in to an impulse and pulled her close. Once she was in his embrace, he felt all the frustrations of his day melt away.

He inhaled the fresh scent of her shampoo as he brushed his cheek over her hair.

"Best part of my day," he said, drawing back.

She smiled up at him, her expression radiant. "Best part of mine, too."

"I didn't call you just to hug you." He laughed then pulled out a chair for her to sit on.

He perched on the edge of the desk across from her as she sat down, tucking her skirt around her legs.

"I asked you to come because I got good news. I just got off the phone with Freddy," Tate continued. "He agreed to drop the lien. I got Benny and him to come to an agreement. Freddy will be signing off on the paperwork this afternoon."

Renee nodded, and Tate was surprised at her restrained response. "This was what you wanted, wasn't it?"

"Yes, of course. It was, but somehow, it doesn't seem as important now that my mother doesn't want to leave for Vancouver."

She lifted one shoulder in a hesitant shrug, as if she didn't dare say more than that.

"And I don't know if I'm stepping over the line here," she continued, "but my mother just told me that she and your father, well, they seem to be in a relationship."

Tate only grinned, thankful that she now knew, as well. "You just preempted me. That was another of the reasons I wanted to talk to you, as well. Dad just told me. They must have made a decision to break the news at the same time. My dad is happier than he's been for a long time."

"My mother, too, but..." Her voice faded away as a frown wrinkled her forehead.

"But what?"

Renee looked directly at him, concern shadowing her face. "Does your father know what he's getting into? As far as my mother's care is concerned?"

Tate felt a hint of foreboding at her tone. "I don't know. We didn't talk about that."

"It's a major concern for me," Renee said.

"Do you think you're the only one who can take care of her?"

Renee's frown deepened, and Tate wished he could take back what he'd just said.

"It isn't just a matter of pushing a wheelchair now and again," Renee said, the anxiety on her face now edging her voice. "It's more than revamping a house to allow it to be accessible.

There are health issues to deal with, daily care. I don't know if he realizes—"

Tate touched her lips with his finger to stop her from saying any more. "He might not know the full extent of your mother's care, but he's a man in love, and he's not irresponsible. I trust that he is going into this with his eyes wide-open."

Renee bit her lip, as if still unconvinced.

"They'll be fine," Tate said. "And I'm sure whatever needs to be done, your mother will tell him, and what she can't tell him, you can."

"I suppose," Renee said, but Tate noted the hesitation in her voice. Then she gave him a quick smile. "It's just that I've been responsible for her care for so long, I can't imagine just handing it over to someone else."

"She's an adult, not a child," Tate reminded her.

Renee laughed. "You're right. I tend to be overprotective." She smiled at him again.

"Now then, I was wondering if you're free on Thursday. There's a play in Calgary I'd like to see."

"My mother and I have a conference call with the therapy team in Vancouver on Thursday at five. I don't think it will take long. I could call you when it's done."

Tate kissed her again. "I'll be praying for you and your mother. Praying that you will be able to live with the decision she makes."

She laid the palm of her hand against his face, her eyes glistening. "You are such a blessing to me. I feel like my life has fallen into a good place."

"I feel the same. I think you need to know that I've never felt this way, even with Molly."

Her smile shone like sunshine breaking through clouds. "I'm so thankful for you," she whispered. "I hope Addison will feel the same."

"I hope so, too."

"When do you think we should talk to her?"

"What do you mean?"

"About us," Renee said, suddenly growing shy. "I'm sure she has some idea of what's going on. Especially after Sunday."

"Yes, I'm sure she does." In fact, Addison had mentioned how much they'd seen of Renee lately. "But I'm not so sure we need to move so quickly on that."

"It's not that quick. Not if...not if things are changing between us."

Tate pulled in a long breath, realizing how this might look to Renee. "Maybe, but I need to be careful with Addison."

"Of course you do, but she's also—" Renee stopped herself.

"Were you going to say that she is also your daughter?" Tate asked.

Renee held her hand up in a gesture of defense. "I was. But that was out of line. I'm sorry."

"Of course," he said.

But what she'd said was the truth. Now that it was spoken, it needed to be addressed.

Renee shook her head. "Please forget I said anything. Addison is... I know she's your daughter first. I have no claim to her..." Renee let the sentence drift away.

Tate wasn't sure how to fix things between them, and when he leaned forward to give her a kiss, she drew away.

"Speaking of responsibilities, I should get back to the store," she said, her voice tight. "I don't like to leave Mom alone too long."

Tate felt the sudden frostiness in Renee's demeanor, and in spite of his confidence that he was doing the right thing, he knew he had hurt her.

He caught her hand and pressed a kiss to her palm. Then, as if to capture it, he curled her fingers around it and pressed them down.

"In case you might need it before we see each other again," he said with a smile.

Renee looked down at her hand. "I won't waste it," she said with a wistful smile.

But she didn't return his kiss as she left.

Tate watched her go, misgivings swimming at the back of his mind. This hadn't gone the way it should have.

But what else was he supposed to do? He cared for Renee more than he had ever cared for anyone else, but Addison was his daughter. He had to watch out for her.

He dragged his hands over his face. He knew he was wise to wait before telling Addison, but at the same time, he felt as if he had made a misstep with Renee that would be hard to undo.

❦

RENEE SAT IN HER OFFICE. Quiet. Alone.

It was Thursday. The day of the conference call with the therapist. The day that she had waited so long for, it was permanently imprinted on her mind.

However, right now all she could think of was Tate and the confusion of emotions he created in her. Tonight they were going out on a date, and while she was excited, a small part of her struggled with her own emotions.

She hadn't been able to stop her sorrow when Tate had said he didn't want to tell Addison about them. While her head understood the wisdom of his words, her heart knew that Tate was holding back. Keeping part of himself separate from her.

And, even more, keeping Addison from her.

He's a father, she reminded herself. *He has to be sure.*

But she's your daughter.

She couldn't lay claim to Addison, though, and therefore, couldn't expect Tate to honor that.

"Are you putting in an order?"

Renee's mother's voice broke into her thoughts.

"We're getting low on glitter, ink, patterned paper, and we could really use some of the new Copic colors," her mother said, hands resting on the wheels of her chair. "Now that we're not selling the store, we're going to need to do a large restock."

"I know. That also means some large bills," Renee said, turning back to her computer screen.

"But the bank account is healthier than it's been in months, so I think we can afford it."

Renee sat back in her chair, smiling at the changes her mother had made to her wardrobe the past few days, including today. The cream-colored T-shirt she wore was new, as were her pants. Her mother had looped a brightly colored scarf around her neck, enhancing the asymmetrical haircut Trudy at Hair Today had talked her into getting.

The highlights glinting in her hair, combined with her clothes, gave her mother a youthful and vibrant look, and as Renee held her mom's shining gaze, she felt a pulse of gratitude for Arlan Truscott. He had given Brenda a shine to her eyes that Renee hadn't seen since her father had been alive.

She was about to say something to her mother, when the front door of the shop flew open, the bell jangling.

"Renee? Renee? Where are you?" a voice called out on a sob.

Renee hurried past her mother, who had already turned to see what was happening. "Addison?"

The little girl stood by the wooden front desk, her backpack slung over one shoulder, her ponytail askew, her cheeks shining with tears as she looked around wildly. She was clutching a book to her chest, and as Renee came closer, she recognized the scrapbook they had made.

"Sweetheart, what's the matter?" Renee hurried to Addison's side.

Addison threw herself into Renee's arms, almost knocking her over, her sobs echoing throughout the store.

A group of younger women, pushing baby buggies, looked their way. Then one of the babies, sensing Addison's distress, started to whimper, as well.

"I'll take care of the customers," her mother said.

Renee nodded, taking the still-sobbing Addison by the hand and leading her to her office. She closed the door behind them, then sat down on a chair and pulled Addison close.

"What's wrong, honey?" Renee asked. "Are you feeling okay? Are you sick? Should we call your dad?"

Addison heaved out a few more sobs, then drew in a shuddering breath as she shook her head.

"Where's Blythe?" Renee prompted.

"She...she's be...behind me," Addison hicupped. She swiped her cheeks with her palm, her other hand still clutching the scrapbook. "I'm supposed to go to her house tonight."

So that Renee and Tate could go on their date, Renee realized.

Renee let the girl settle down a moment, then eased her into the chair beside her, grabbing the box of tissues from the desk.

"Tell me what's wrong," she said, tugging a couple free and gently wiping the little girl's eyes. Her heart broke for her, and she wondered if she was missing her mother.

Addison sniffed again, then looked down at the book she clung to. "My friends are mean," was all she said.

"How are they mean?"

"I brought my scrapbook to school to show my teacher. Then my friends wanted to see it, so I showed them. My one friend said that her mommy took lots and lots of pictures of her in the hospital and that I didn't have any pictures of me inside the hospital, so I told her I was adop...adopted." Addison released another whimpering sob.

"But, honey, you've always known you were adopted," Renee said, unable to quench the usual quiver of regret at the reality.

"I know, but my friend said that my mommy, my biological mommy, didn't want me. That she gave me away."

Addison's words stabbed at Renee's heart with swift, sure strokes.

"But you know better, don't you?" Renee asked, her words tentative, unsure in the face of this girl's sobbing grief.

Addison looked up at Renee, her teary gaze creating a deathly chill in Renee's soul.

"My friend said my real mommy gave me away because she didn't love me."

Renee blanched at the cold, hard anger in Addison's voice.

Addison's eyes grew narrow as Renee pulled herself together. "My other friend said that my mommy is probably still alive." Addison drew in another quick breath, hitting the floor with her toes, her anger building with each kick of her black school shoes.

Renee struggled to find words to help this sweet little girl. "I'm sure your real mommy had her reasons. Sometimes mommies can't take care—"

"I hate my real mom," Addison spat out, cutting off Renee's explanation. "She didn't love me. I hope I never have to see her. Ever. I hate her."

Renee fell back against the chair, her world whirling around her with each bit of venom coming from her daughter's lips.

She tried to breathe, couldn't catch enough air.

Then the door to the office opened, and Blythe poked her head inside.

"There you are, you stinker," she said to Addison in a teasing singsong voice at odds with the heavy atmosphere in the room. "We should go. I have to help my mother with some grocery shopping before we go to my place."

Addison sniffled and stood up. Then without a backward glance at Renee, she left.

I hate my real mommy.

Those five words dragged out all the guilt and pain and sorrow that had been bottled up for years.

Renee pressed ice-cold hands to her face, trying to center herself, struggling to know how to handle all her emotions.

Swirling through the center of them was one thought.

Tate was right.

She was glad they hadn't told Addison.

Was that only a few minutes ago that she had so looked forward to seeing Tate? Was that flash of happiness the last one she would ever experience? She was dimly aware of the noises beyond the back room, her head still ringing with Addison's words.

"Renee?"

Her mother tapping at the office door broke into Renee's jumbled thoughts. She blinked and inhaled, not wanting Brenda to see her anguish. "What is it?"

The door opened and her mom wheeled herself inside, frowning at Renee. "What's going on? Why are you hiding in here? Where's Addison? I thought you were still talking with her."

Renee held up one hand, forestalling further questions. "Not now, Mom."

"What do you mean, 'not now'? You've been sitting here for over twenty minutes. I thought you were busy in here with Addison, and now I see she's gone."

"She left with Blythe," Renee said, surprised she could still speak.

"Tate called a few moments ago. He said something about your date tonight? You should probably call him back."

Why hadn't he asked to talk to her?

Had Addison gone to his office and told him the same thing?

I hate her.

If it came down to that, she knew who Tate would choose.

Brenda wheeled herself into the office and closed the door. "Renee, what is going on?"

"It doesn't matter." Renee got up and brushed her pants, as if brushing off the memories that clung to her.

"It does. I can see you're upset. I haven't seen you this upset since..."

"The accident?" Renee finished for her.

Brenda shook her head. "No. Since I asked you what happened to your baby."

Another shock trickled like ice down Renee's spine. She and her mother seldom spoke of that day, when her mother had come out of her coma after the accident. After Addison's birth. The first thing Brenda had asked Renee was where her baby was. Renee hadn't answered, and Addison had never come up again. It was as if they'd silently agreed to leave that topic buried.

"Renee, please tell me what's going on," her mother pleaded. "I feel like this is all connected to Addison and Tate somehow. Tell me. Please."

Renee could taste the words on her tongue.

Addison is my daughter. Your granddaughter.

"No. I can't," was all she could say.

Then a peculiar expression washed over her mom's face.

"She's your girl, isn't she?" she said, her voice tight with suppressed emotion. "Addison is the baby you gave up for adoption. She's my granddaughter."

Renee stared at her mother, wishing she could tell her no.

Then Brenda caught her by the hand, her fingers strong and hard. "Don't deny it. I've always felt a strong connection to her, and you're not saying no. Why couldn't I see it?"

Renee wanted to deny it, but she couldn't contain the information anymore. "Because she looks more like Dwight than me," Renee said, her voice quiet.

"Were you and Tate ever going to tell her?"

"No. Tate and I didn't talk about that."

"What did you talk about?"

About me wanting to tell Addison about us.

Too easily she remembered Tate's hesitation, and though she understood it, she also felt as if she didn't matter to him. Well, apparently, she didn't matter to her daughter, either.

"You need to call Tate. To find out what's going on," her mother urged. "You need to talk about Addison."

Renee thought back to Addison's angry words, and she felt the sorrow rising in her throat. She couldn't cry. Not now. "Please stop telling me what to do with my life," she snapped.

"Why not? You've spent eight years telling me what to do with mine."

Renee just stared at her, feeling as if her mother had just slapped her.

"It's always been for you," Renee said. "Everything I've ever done has been about you getting better."

Her mother, still holding on to her hand, shook her head. "No. It's been for you. Everything that we've done, all the plans we've made the past year, have been about you trying to erase your guilt."

"How can you say that?" Renee asked, the pain rising to the surface. "I thought this therapy program was what you wanted, too."

"At first, maybe, but I agreed with all the plans, the appointments, the hoping and dreaming, because I thought it was the only way you would forgive yourself. For a while I wanted it, too, but for your sake more than mine. I could see how the guilt consumed you. Then I realized I was allowed to put myself first, and in the past few weeks I had a reason to. I don't want to go to Vancouver anymore. Not if it means moving away from Arlan and Addison. My granddaughter."

Her mother's claim on the little girl sent a fresh wave of sorrow coursing through Renee.

"If you really cared about me, you would have told me about Addison when you found out," her mother continued, her voice heavy with desolation. "I lost more than my ability to walk in that accident. I lost my grandchild. And that's always bothered me more than this wheelchair has."

"I had no right to tell you about her," Renee said. "I gave up that right when I walked away from the hospital. I gave her up because I needed to take care of you. Everything I did was so you could become the person you deserved to be. I thought if I could see you walk again, the sacrifice I made would be worthwhile. But she's not my daughter now. She's Tate's."

"She's always been your daughter," Brenda said. "Always will be."

Renee felt as if she was falling into a hurricane of sorrow and anguish. She needed some room to breathe, to think.

"I'm sorry, Mom. I can't talk about this anymore." She was about to walk away, when her mother called her name.

"What about Tate?" she asked. "What do I tell him when he calls?"

Renee stopped, clutching her midsection. "Nothing. Don't tell him anything. Please, just do that much for me. Don't tell Tate and please don't approach Addison."

Then she walked out of the store and down the street. How could she think about being with Tate now?

Addison was everything to him. He protected her and cared for her.

And to Addison, Renee was nothing.

CHAPTER THIRTEEN

*T*ate dropped his phone onto the cradle, leaned back in his office chair and shoved his hands through his hair. Renee hadn't answered her phone for the past two hours.

Mrs. Albertson wouldn't tell him what was happening when he went to the store. The only thing she would say was that Renee was upset and needed some space.

Had she changed her mind about them? Was she having second thoughts?

He thought back to that moment in the office. After he had told her he didn't want Addison to know about them yet.

She had pulled away, created a distance. And she hadn't spoken to him since.

He turned back to his computer, trying to focus on what was on the screen, when his cell phone buzzed. Renee. Finally.

He drew in a steady breath and forced a light and cheerful tone to his voice. "Hey. How's it going?"

All he heard on her end was a sniff, and dread curled through his stomach.

"Are you okay? Did something happen?"

"I'm okay. I'm just..." Another sniff followed.

"Just what? Did you hurt yourself?"

"No. No. Nothing like that." She drew in a long breath. "I won't be going out with you tonight."

"Why not? Did something else come up?"

"Sort of." She released a bitter laugh, and his stomach churned. "And that's why tonight isn't happening."

"What do you mean, 'isn't happening'? Do you want to do it another night? Tomorrow?"

"No...no. I don't know."

Her hesitation scared him. "Are you upset with me because I didn't want to tell Addison about us?"

"No. It's a good thing you didn't. Not now."

Tate tried to wrap his head around what she was saying, wishing he could see her face and decipher her emotions. "Where are you? We need to talk about this."

"No. There's nothing to talk about."

"I can't believe that," he said, pressing his fingers to his pounding temples. "What aren't you telling me?"

Silence rose up between them.

"I can't be what you want me to be," Renee finally said. "And I can't be what Addison needs. This will never work."

Icy dread shivered down his spine, and his stomach clenched. *No. Not again.* Memories of Molly's betrayal taunted him.

You were left behind once before. Are you going to let it happen again?

Behind that question came a deluge of anger. How could Renee have done this to him, to his daughter? How could she have let herself become a part of their life, then pull away? He had been so careful with his own heart and even more cautious with Addison's.

And now?

"So just like that? You're giving up on me?"

She didn't say anything.

How was he supposed to react to her silence? He had dared to think he could make future plans with her. Plans that included Addison. Her daughter.

"I just need...to get away for a while."

Away for a while. Exactly what Molly had told him when he had discovered she was cheating on him. Why did the women in his life seem to think that problems could be resolved by running away?

But this time he wasn't going to sit idly by. He wasn't going to be the one sitting and waiting. And this time he was going to protect his daughter with everything in him.

"Is it just me you need to get away from, or is Addison part of this, too?"

"In a way—"

"So you're giving up on her, too," he said, knowing he was unleashing destruction by using words in anger. But he couldn't stop himself. "You're giving up on her again."

Her gasp of pain made him instantly regret what he had said, but he couldn't bring the words back. He waited a moment, trying to find a way to connect with her.

"I guess this is goodbye, then," was all she said, followed by a faint click.

The conversation was over. She was gone.

He tossed the cell phone on the desk.

What had just happened?

He got up to stand by the window, his hands resting on his hips. From here he saw Evangeline's bookstore across the street, the flower shop beside it. Beyond them, the road snaking upward to a subdivision overlooking the town where Renee and her mother lived.

He rested his forehead against the cool glass, trying to gather his scattered senses.

Renee had just ended their relationship. It was over.

He straightened, rolled his sleeves down and buttoned his

cuffs. He turned back to his desk and closed the file he had been working on.

Then he grabbed his jacket, stabbed his hands in the sleeves and settled it over his shoulders.

It was over.

Now he knew he had been right to trust his intuition not to tell Addison.

Would things have gone differently between him and Renee if he had?

He shook his head, sensing that something else was going on. Brenda Albertson wouldn't tell him, and he knew he wouldn't be talking to Renee anytime soon.

Now what?

He turned off his computer, grabbed his briefcase and headed down the stairs and out into the street. It was close to suppertime. Shops were closing down for the day and traffic was easing off.

He glanced down the street to the scrapbook store and noticed the Closed sign on the door. Renee was obviously gone, as well.

Thinking of her made his heart hurt. That was the only way to describe what was happening to him. It was a pain that reminded him of the first time he'd realized his relationship with Molly was unraveling.

But with Renee, it hurt more. He couldn't understand it. He had been with Molly ten years, Renee only a few weeks.

But Renee affected him in a way Molly never had. They had connected in ways he and Molly never had.

She was a woman of God.

He sighed, and walked back to the parking lot where his truck was parked. Addison was staying at Blythe's place. His father was out for the night with Mrs. Albertson. He was on his own.

Making a quick decision, he put the truck in gear and

headed home. Once there he quickly changed into his blue jeans, shirt and jacket, then headed up to Evangeline's ranch.

Half an hour later, Tate and his horse, Duke, were heading up into the hills. The steady beat of Duke's hooves was the only sound. He heard the occasional hum of a vehicle on the road, and then, after twenty minutes, even that was muted to nothing.

He broke out into the open field and dismounted, leading Duke to a tree. He tossed the reins over a branch, knowing it was enough to keep the horse close by, then sat down at the base of the tree, leaning back against it, looking out over the valley. He glanced over at the mountain overlooking Rockyview, trying to find the Shadow Woman Renee had pointed out on their ride together. A woman waiting for her lost love to return.

He stared, waiting as the sun drifted down the sky, and then he saw it. Just as Renee had said. A face and then the body, leaning forward. Waiting.

He doubted Renee was waiting for him. She was the one who had pushed him away.

He knew he hadn't helped the situation, but he'd been trying to protect his heart from breaking. He couldn't go through that again as he had with Molly.

Thank goodness he hadn't told his daughter about his relationship with Renee. His heartbreak was hard enough to handle. He couldn't imagine what it would have done to Addison.

I can't be what Addison needs. I can't be what you need.

No matter how many times he went over the conversation with Renee, he kept coming back to those puzzling words.

He laid his head back against the tree as the sun began to slip behind the mountains, the sudden cooler air washing over him.

He closed his eyes. *Dear Lord, I don't know what to think. Don't know what to do. I trusted Renee. I cared for her. I was ready to make her a permanent part of my life. But now...*

Show me what to do, Lord. Help me to trust in You. Help me to be a good father to Addison. To be the father she needs.

His priority had always been Addison. He had to put her needs before his own.

Blessedly, he wasn't completely alone. He could go on in God's strength.

It would still be difficult. Renee had found a place in his heart that no woman had before. How was he ever going to fill that hole again?

‹‹‹›››

"So TELL me again what he said?" Evangeline asked, scraping a chair across the wooden floor to join Renee at the old, worn table that had belonged to Evangeline's mother.

"He said I was giving up on him. Him and Addison." Renee leaned her elbows on the table, turning her head to look out the window, hoping to hide the sorrow in her eyes.

Evangeline, like Mia, lived above her store in an apartment with windows overlooking Main Street. Renee could see her scrapbook store and Tate's office.

Thinking of him sent a pain through her midsection.

After her conversation with Tate, she had come here. Evangeline had taken one look at Renee, put a Closed sign in the door and brought her upstairs to her apartment.

"Why did he say that?" Evangeline's voice held a harsh note, completely at odds with her friend's sunny and happy nature. "You've been so careful with Addison—how could he say you're giving up on her? What a cad."

In spite of her sadness, Renee couldn't stop a smile at her friend's old-fashioned phrasing.

"He's not the cad, exactly," Renee said, grabbing the cup of coffee she'd been nursing the past few minutes.

"So what happened?"

"It was a bad combination of events." Renee looked down at the liquid floating in the ceramic mug. "I know he was trying to protect Addison when he didn't want to tell her about us, and he was right."

"Okay, but why do I feel like there's something missing here, between him not wanting to tell Addison about you and you not thinking this will work?"

"It's such a tangle. I feel as if my life's been broken apart," Renee continued, sidestepping Evangeline's question. "Everything I thought I could count on has been stripped away. My mom doesn't want to do the new therapy program, and we missed the conference call this afternoon, and this thing between me and Tate—it's just not going to work. How could everything have come apart so quickly?"

"And you hate chaos," Evangeline said quietly. "So can't you talk to him?"

Renee shook her head. "Talking isn't going to fix anything. Not now."

Evangeline sighed. "I had such high hopes. He's the perfect man for you."

Renee gave her friend a wistful smile. "I should have known it was too good to be true."

"You're allowed to be happy, you know," Evangeline said.

"What do you mean by that?"

Evangeline shrugged. "You've put your mother's needs ahead of yours for so long, I don't think you know how to live for yourself, how to embrace happiness. Just don't give up on Tate too quickly." Evangeline smiled at her, then squeezed her hand. "Maybe you need to pray about this."

Renee gave her friend a puzzled look. "You haven't been to church in a while and you're telling me to pray?"

Evangeline shrugged. "I know your relationship with God is solid. You'll probably find comfort in praying."

Renee held Evangeline's sincere gaze, then nodded. "You're

probably right."

How often had she sought to take care of things on her own, only to discover that she needed to depend on God? That only He could give her everything she needed and only He could make all things well.

"Sometimes I am," Evangeline said with a grin.

The jangling ring of her phone broke into the sanctity and silence of the moment, and for a few seconds Renee was tempted to ignore it.

But then she remembered the conference call.

She yanked her phone out of her purse, but the number displayed wasn't from the therapist.

It was Cathy Meckle. The potential buyer of the store.

She shot Evangeline an apologetic glance. "Sorry. I should take this."

Evangeline waved off her concern. "I'll be downstairs if you need me."

"Thanks. Hey?" Renee quickly said before she answered the phone call. "You're a dear friend."

Evangeline waved off her thanks, then left.

"Renee, I haven't heard from you for a while." Cathy's perky voice echoed on the other line. "I was wondering how things are progressing. With the lien and everything?"

"Um, good. Uh, the lien is off the store."

"That's marvelous. So that means we can progress with the sale?"

"I hadn't heard from you for a while so I wasn't sure—"

"I know. I know. And I'm sorry. Things have been crazy, but they're settling down now."

Lucky you, Renee thought.

"And I have to confess, I was getting impatient. I had been looking at another store, but I realized that Rockyview is such a perfect place to settle down and raise our kids. We found the perfect house there, and Ned got a job in Highview, which isn't far away, so we decided to go ahead with our initial plan and buy the store."

"You know, things have been really busy," Renee said quietly. "Can you give me a day to get things in order and I'll call you back?"

"Sure. Of course. I just want you to know that we're pretty definite on this, so I hope you haven't found anyone else."

"No. You would get first chance at it," Renee said, her mind still reeling. "Thanks so much for calling. We'll stay in touch."

Cathy said goodbye, reiterated how much she wanted to buy the store and then, finally, hung up.

Renee dropped her phone, then walked to the window and looked down at the store she and her mother had begun all those years ago. Only a month ago she'd had plans to leave this place, and though her heart hadn't been in it, she'd clung to the hope offered by the therapy program for her mother.

But could she stay now?

The man she had thought she loved had pushed her away.

You were the one who pushed him away. You told him you didn't know if this would work.

All she had been doing was expressing her own fears and insecurities. And then he told her she was betraying Addison. Again.

And maybe she was, but one thing she knew for certain; she couldn't stay here anymore. Not in the same town as her daughter.

The daughter of a man she thought she loved.

She took mental stock of her situation, her mind listing all the pros and cons.

She needed some time away from town, away from the possibility of running into Tate. But how was she supposed to do that? Her mother still needed daily care.

Suddenly, she had an idea. She called the store and Ashley answered.

"I have a huge favor to ask you," she said, looking out over the street. "Would you be able to mind the store with my mother for the next couple of days?"

"Of course I can. I'm not really busy, so that works out perfect."

"I know it's a super short notice, but I need a couple days away from the store." She could head down to Banff, one of her favorite retreat spots. Maybe do some hiking. She'd been meaning to head up to the tea house, but she'd never had the time.

"That's just fine. Will your mother be needing any help?"

"I'll be home in the evenings," Renee said. From the way things were progressing with her mother and Arlan, she didn't need to worry about Brenda being lonely, either.

But could she leave?

Don't think about that now, she told herself. *Take it one step at a time. Go away for a while. Give yourself some space.*

Yet, even as she grabbed her purse and headed down the back stairs to leave, deep in her lonely soul, she knew exactly what she had to do.

CHAPTER FOURTEEN

"*A*re you busy? Can I come in?"

Tate looked up from his computer. His father stood in the doorway of his office. "Of course you can," he said.

Arlan closed the door behind him, then ambled into Tate's office. "This is a good place," he said. "A good place for a family."

Tate pushed his shirtsleeves up his arms and leaned back in his chair. He guessed this was a preamble to what his father really wanted to talk about, so he just waited.

His father slipped his hands into his pockets and leaned back against the wall behind him.

"What's troubling you, Dad?" Tate asked, giving Arlan an opening. "I'm thinking it isn't the lease agreement you've been struggling with for that new development on the edge of town."

"Actually I think there's more that's troubling you."

"What do you mean?"

"I had a visit this morning while you were at Addison's play. From Renee. She's putting the scrapbook store up for sale."

Why did that send a sliver of dread through him?

"Probably for the best," he said, trying to sound more casual than he felt, trying to still the pounding of his heart.

"Why do you say that?"

Tate swiveled his chair back and forth, back and forth. "It's an awkward situation. What with Addison and all."

"And you and all," Arlan added.

Tate shrugged. The past few days had been empty and lonely. He hated the way he felt, and hated that Renee had made him feel this way. He had been so careful to guard his heart, but she had burst through his defenses.

"She's selling the store because she doesn't want to cause problems for you and Addison. I can't think of a more unselfish and admirable act."

Tate didn't know what to say.

"She looks incredibly sad," his father continued. "I don't think it's because she's selling the store, though."

Tate missed Renee more than he thought possible, but where to start? "So what am I supposed to do?" he asked.

"I think you should go talk to her."

"We tried talking," he said. "That didn't end well."

"And you're going to leave it at that? What kind of lawyer are you to let someone walk all over you?"

Tate acknowledged his father's attempt at humor with a wry smile. "I've spent enough of my married life running after a woman, trying to placate her. Trying to figure out what she really wanted. I can't...I can't do it again."

"Can't or won't?"

Tate sucked in an angry breath. "I have to take care of Addison."

"At this point, I think taking care of Addison involves trying to find a way to make things work between you and Renee," Arlan continued.

"A few days ago, when all this fell apart, I went up to the mountains," Tate said. "I prayed that God would help me be a good father. And from what Renee told me, that involves leaving her alone. She pretty much told me that she can't be a good mother to Addison. I can't put Addison through that again, no matter how much it hurts me."

His father nodded, as if slowly weighing what he was saying. "As a father, you should put Addison first. But why do you think Renee said what she did? About not being able to be the mother Addison needed?"

Tate shrugged. "I don't know. I...I got upset. I told her that she had given up on Addison once and that she was doing it again."

"You didn't!"

His father's shocked voice only underlined Tate's own shame at what he had said.

"I was angry, upset and afraid. I'm responsible for Addison, and I take that seriously. Especially after Molly's haphazard mothering."

"I don't want to preach at you, but I think you need to know that while Addison is your daughter, she is God's child first." His father gave him a lopsided smile. "It's not completely on your shoulders to do everything for her."

Tate nodded, and his father continued, "I think you need to find out what Renee meant when she said she didn't think she could be the mother Addison needed."

Tate dragged his hands over his face, his fingers rasping on the whiskers he hadn't bothered to shave this morning. Then he looked up at his father. "Why do I get the feeling that you already have a good idea why?"

"A good lawyer never approaches a case without knowing all the facts," was Arlan's vague reply.

"So tell me."

"It's Renee's story to tell."

"Humor me," Tate said, an edge of impatience entering his voice.

His father cocked an eyebrow at him, but he shifted his shoulder. "She compared herself to Molly. I'm sure there's more that she didn't tell me, but she has the idea that Molly was an exemplary mother, and she didn't think she could measure up."

"I think she got that idea from working on the scrapbook. I was always talking Molly up." Tate eased out a sigh. "But you said you think there's more?"

"That's just a notion I have. The only way you'll find out is by talking to Renee yourself."

Did he want to go there? Did he want to open himself up to more pain if Renee was only hiding behind what she said as an excuse to keep him and Addison away?

"She's worth taking a chance on," his father continued. "The fact that she's willing to sacrifice the store, first for her mother and then for Addison and you, should show you what an amazing woman Renee is."

Shame licked at him. His father was right. What they had together was worth taking a chance on. Besides, how could he feel any worse than he did now?

He glanced at the clock, and his father waved him off. "Don't worry about Addison," he said. "I'll keep her entertained when she comes here from school."

"Okay." He rolled down his sleeves and ran his hands over his hair in an attempt to neaten it.

"You look fine," his father assured him. "Now go. I'm sure Renee is at the store, even though it looks closed. Her mother told me."

With a quick smile at his father and a prayer on his lips, Tate strode out of the office and down the stairs before he talked himself out of this.

He came to the store. A large For Sale sign was placed in the window, the reality of what his father had said sinking in. She really was leaving.

He peered into the shop and, thankfully, didn't notice anyone inside. He watched for a few moments, ignoring the people who walked past him, shooting him curious glances.

Probably wondering why he was stalking Scrap Happy.

He didn't see any movement in the store.

The Closed sign hung in the door, but when he tested the doorknob, he found it was unlocked. He slowly opened the door, being careful not to disturb the bells that announced the entrance of a customer. As he stepped inside, he glanced around.

Still empty.

He walked quietly past the counter, looking toward the back. He could just make out the room where he and Addison and Renee had worked on Molly's scrapbook together. The one that had caused so many problems.

Then he saw Renee. She sat at the table. He quietly returned to the front door and locked it.

Taking a deep breath, he walked quietly to the back of the store.

Renee sat at the table, her Bible open in front of her.

He paused a moment, watching as she picked up a piece of paper from beside the Bible and held it up.

His heart shifted in his chest when he recognized a picture of him and Addison. It must have been one of the discards. Probably because Molly wasn't in it.

He heard a sniffle, then he saw her lift a finger and slowly, gently trace his face. The look of yearning on her features made his heart skip. Then the picture fluttered out of her fingers as she dropped her face into her palms, her shoulders shaking with quiet sobs.

The sight tore at his heart.

He sent up another prayer for wisdom, then knocked lightly on the door.

She grabbed a tissue and dabbed her eyes, then said, "Can I help you?"

As her eyes met his, her face lost all color, her eyes widened and her mouth fell open.

Then, as if a shutter fell across her features, her expression shifted, erasing any vestige of the emotion he had just seen on her face.

"What are you doing here?"

Her question came out in a rush of confusion.

Tate found himself unable to speak. Seeing Renee sitting there, looking at the picture of him and Addison with such stark emotion, melted the ice that had encased his heart the past few days. His father was right. She was withholding some vital piece of evidence.

"We need to talk."

She picked up the crumpled tissue that lay at her elbow and swiped at her eyes. "There's not much to say."

He decided to push forward. "Tell me what you meant when you said you couldn't be the kind of mother Addison needed. What kind of mother do you think she needs?"

Renee's mouth was set in a stubborn line, and for a moment Tate didn't think she was going to answer him.

"Can we go for a walk to the river?" he asked. He didn't want to sit here in the store, in her territory, so to speak. They needed to find neutral ground.

"I don't know." She glanced at his shoes as if to find a reason to say no.

He held up his foot, showing her the worn cowboy boots he'd started wearing. "You're wearing running shoes and capris. You should be okay."

To his surprise she gave him a careful smile, then, thankfully, she nodded. "I'll just lock up, and we can go out the back door."

"The front door is locked already."

"Okay. Let's go." She led him out the back door and into the bright sunshine.

They walked down the alley, then the street leading away from Main Street and toward the river that flowed through town.

A light breeze blew through her hair as they walked. Each step eased the tension in Tate's shoulders.

"How's your mother?" he asked finally, needing to ease them into some kind of conversation.

"I haven't seen her this happy in years." She gave him a cautious smile. "How about your dad?"

"Ditto," Tate said.

They turned a corner and walked down a narrow road toward the park that ran along the river. Renee turned off the road onto a path that beckoned through trees.

"I've never been here," Tate said.

"You'll just have to trust me not to lead you wrong."

Tate was quiet a moment. "That's probably been part of my problem," he said.

"What do you mean?" Renee asked.

He slipped his hands into the pockets of his jeans, glancing sidelong at her, disconcerted to see her watching him. "I didn't trust our relationship enough," he said. "Not enough to tell Addison about us."

They turned another corner, and Tate heard the river spilling over rocks.

"You had your reasons," she said as she pushed aside some branches and then stepped onto a gravel bar that ran along the river.

"But she's your daughter, too, and I was getting confused about where we fit in your life. Everything kept blurring together."

Renee laughed. "Life isn't like that. You don't make compartments. Addison here, me there, you there. Relationships are like a web, intricate and connected. You are her father, and, yes, she's my daughter, but our relationship is...was—" She stopped there, uncertainty entering her voice.

"I'm hoping for 'is,'" Tate finished for her.

She said nothing, her hands swinging loosely beside her as

she walked to a large log beached on the gravel bar. For a moment he thought he had truly managed to mess things up for good between them.

"I'm sorry," he said finally. "I'm sorry about what I said. About you giving up on Addison. That was wrong. I was afraid and I wanted to be in control of the situation."

Renee sat on the log, lowering her head, her hair falling around her face. Was she crying again? He caught her chin under his hand, lifting her face to his. Though he saw pain there, her eyes were dry.

"Enough dancing around," he said. "Why did you tell me you couldn't be what Addison needed? What I needed?"

Renee held his gaze a moment, then gently pulled her head away, looking up at the mountains surrounding the town. "You can see the Shadow Woman," was all she said.

Tate frowned, but looked where she was pointing. And he saw her clearly this time.

Then Renee lowered her hand, picked up a rock and, with a flick of her wrist, sent it skipping a couple of times over the surface of the water.

"It was what Addison said to me," she finally replied.

"What did she say? When?" Tate's confusion only grew at her cryptic answer.

"She came to the store when I called you. She was upset and crying. One of her friends had told her that her biological mother must not have loved her and that's why she gave Addison up. Addison was upset, understandably, and she told me that she hated her biological mother. Who is me." Her voice quivered.

Tate sucked in a quick breath, his hands coming to rest on her shoulders, tightening their grip as if protecting her. "Why would she say that?"

"I couldn't separate what she said from me. And I couldn't be in a relationship with you, knowing that Addison, the person you love more than life itself, thought that way about me."

"She wasn't talking about you, Renee Albertson. She was talking about her unknown mother. Not you."

"But I was the one who walked away from her, as you said."

Tate winced. "I'm so sorry I said that. I didn't know Addison had said that to you. Besides, what choice did you have? You were all alone. Your mother was sick, and she couldn't have helped you."

"Lots of young mothers don't have help," she said in a choked voice. "They manage somehow."

"But your mother needed you, too. You couldn't do both, and you weren't going to do a halfway job of taking care of Addison. You are the kind of person who is either all in or all out. You have done amazing things for your mother. That store you have—I don't know many daughters who can work with their mother half as well as you do. That's not just guilt that's motivating you—that's a genuine and true love for your mother that I admire."

Renee looked up at him, her eyes alight with a wonder that gave him hope. "You sound like you're defending me."

He let his grip loosen, his hands lightly caressing her arms. "Maybe I am defending you. You didn't walk out on Addison. I was speaking from a place of hurt and anger. Molly put me through the wringer with her cheating, and I wasn't going to allow myself to go through that again."

"What are you talking about?"

Tate bent over and picked up a handful of rocks, tossing them one at a time into the river that flowed past as he struggled to find the right words to explain his life to her.

"That scrapbook you made for Addison—it was a way of me helping her get through her grief at losing Molly, but it was also a way to sugarcoat a relationship that had never been good."

The rocks fell into the river with faint plops, sending up a light spray of water.

"But the pictures? The trips?" Renee sounded puzzled. "Molly seemed like such a perfect mother. I spent hours trying not to compare myself to her."

"You are nothing like her."

"What are you saying?"

Tate tossed the last of his rocks into the river, creating another spray that was just as quickly erased by the relentless movement of the water.

He gave Renee a wistful smile. "There's Scrapbook Molly and then there's Real Molly. After Molly died, Addison was so heartbroken. I thought the scrapbook would be a way of honoring Addison's memories of Molly. True or not."

"You had some wonderful memories. All those trips. All those things you did for her." Renee's voice grew wistful. "Things I knew I could never have given to her."

Tate took her hand in his, tracing the line of her fingers, trying to connect with her, reassure her. "Those trips and birthdays and Christmases make a good scrapbook, but not a good life. Molly was unhappy and difficult to live with. She was an erratic mother at best, and an unfaithful wife. When she was killed in that accident, I felt so incredibly guilty. We were planning to separate, and after Molly died, I was thankful Addison didn't have to go through that trauma. Addison grieved Molly, as any daughter would her mother." He looked up at her, hoping she understood. "But Molly wasn't the mother portrayed in that scrapbook Addison treasures so much."

Tate touched her face, letting his fingers run down the line of her cheek. "You've shown more consistent mothering to her than Molly ever did. You have a way with her that I don't. I know sometimes it seemed like I resented what you did with her, but that was because I was trying to keep Addison to myself."

"And you were right to do so."

"Maybe at one time, but not anymore. You've become an important part of my life. I haven't been very happy without you."

Renee was silent, and for a moment he thought maybe he had truly messed things up.

"I know I was wrong to keep you at arm's length," he continued, pressing his case. "I was foolishly trying to protect myself. I'm so sorry I said what I did."

Renee shook her head, and when she cupped his face, he felt the tension that had been gripping him ease. Did he still have a chance with her?

"You were just being a good father, and that makes me admire and...care for you even more. Yes, she's my daughter, but you are also the man...the man I love."

Tate's heart faltered. Had she truly said that?

He pulled her close, lowered his head to hers, and as their lips met, he felt as if they were meant to be together. Always.

She pulled back, a look of amazement on her face. "I've had my own struggles," she said. "And I think...I didn't think I was allowed to be so happy. However, you've made me feel like all the decisions in my life, all the missteps, were worth it if it brought you into my life."

"It wouldn't have happened if you hadn't given Addison up all those years ago."

Renee's eyes grew wide with wonder, and she laughed aloud.

Then she threw her arms around Tate and returned his kiss.

"I want to go pick up Addison from school," Tate said. "Together. I want to tell her about us."

He saw a tear slide down Renee's cheek.

"And when we do that, I want to tell her that you are her mother."

He saw hesitation on Renee's face, and he gave her another

quick kiss of consolation. "It will be fine," he assured her. "She loves you, Renee Albertson." He gave her an assuring smile.

"Okay, then," she said with a breathless voice. "Let's do it."

He nodded, then got up and took her hand, pulling her to her feet. Then together they walked away. But as they drove to the school, Tate wondered himself how Addison would react.

❦

RENEE COULDN'T STOP the fear that gripped her as they parked by the school. Though she knew she had a connection with Addison and her daughter cared for her, their relationship was one of friends.

What would Addison say to Renee being her mother? How would she react after the anger she had displayed against the amorphous figure of her natural mother?

"It'll be okay," Tate said, gripping her ice-cold hand in a gesture of reassurance. "Why don't you stay here? I'll go get her and we can take her to the park. Tell her some place private."

Renee nodded, pulling in a deep breath, sending up another prayer.

Tate got out of the car and walked toward the school. It was as if each step pulled him further away from her. What would they do if Addison was upset? What would happen if Addison rejected her?

She couldn't go there. Couldn't focus on that. She and Tate had just gone through a difficult adjustment, a hard time. It had to be for something.

Each minute Tate was gone felt like an hour. Every time a man came walking out of the school with a little girl beside him her heart jumped. She couldn't sit so she got out, pacing back and forth on the sidewalk.

Finally, after eons, Tate appeared, Addison's pink backpack slung over his shoulder. Addison was holding his hand, skipping along, laughing at something he was saying. And when she saw Renee she ran toward her, her smile growing wider.

"You came too?" Addison said catching Renee's hand, glancing back at her father, eyes sparkling. "Both of you came to get me from school?"

"Yes. We wanted to make today special," Tate said.

Over Addison's head, Renee caught his smile but she read the tension in it, which ratcheted up hers.

"What are we doing?" Addison asked as she got into the car and buckled up. Tate put her backpack on the seat beside her then got in and buckled up as well.

"We're going to get some ice cream from Rockyview Creamery and then go for a walk by the river," Tate said as he started up the car and pulled past the school busses, into the stream of other parents picking up kids from school.

"Can I get Tiger ice cream?" Addison asked.

"You can get any kind you want," Tate said, glancing first at Addison then over at Renee.

She wasn't sure she could eat a single thing and when they got out at the Creamery, she turned down the offer of a cone, her entire body tense with a mixture of anticipation and worry.

"You don't like ice cream?" Addison asked as she licked on the orange and black confection she had gotten.

"Usually I do," Renee said, reaching out and taking Addison's hand as they walked past the outdoor tables of the Creamery, heading toward the walking path along the river.

"But not today?" Addison pressed, swinging Renee's hand with a familiarity and ease that gave Renee some reassurance.

"Not today."

"But my dad said it was a special day," Addison pressed, licking a smear of ice cream that ended up on one side of her mouth.

"It is a special day," Tate said, stopping by a bench that over-looked a bend in the river. He sat down and Renee and Addison joined him.

The wood of the bench was warm and the chatter of the river falling over the rocks created a soothing rhythm. Renee was content to let the silence go on but knew Addison would wonder why they were here.

They sat there until Tate and Addison were done their ice cream, but each moment created an increasing tension in Renee. Finally Addison was done. Renee took a package of wipes from her purse and handed her one. Then Tate.

He tossed them in the garbage can beside the bench, then turned to Addison.

"You know, sweetheart, that Renee and I have been spending a lot of time together."

Addison gave Tate a knowing look. "I do. I know you kissed her."

"What? How?" Tate frowned and Renee's thoughts ticked back, wondering when she might have seen them.

"You had some lipstick on your cheek once," Addison said, swinging her legs, looking worldy-wise. "And I know how you look at Renee. I know you like her lots."

Renee couldn't stop the blush warming her cheeks.

"Okay then. Maybe this isn't such a surprise," Tate continued, shooting Renee a quick smile, "but Renee and I are in love and we want to spend more time together. In fact, we want to get married someday."

"Really? For true?" Addison jumped up from the bench and threw herself at Renee, hugging her hard.

"Yes, it's for true."

"Does that mean you're going to be my mom?" Addison asked.

"Yes. It does," Renee said, her love for her daughter filling her heart.

"I am so, so, super excited." Addison squealed, then gave Renee another hug. "I love you so much."

Renee held her close, closing her eyes, embracing her daughter, her emotions bittersweet, clinging to this moment of innocence.

They weren't done yet and from the melancholy look on Tate's face she knew it was time to tell Addison the rest.

"I love you too," Renee said, cradling her daughter's face in her hands and daring to brush a gentle kiss over her forehead. She knew they had to tread carefully now, weigh each word. "In fact, I...I have always loved you."

"Always?" Addison released a light laugh, looking surprised. "You've only known me for a little while."

Renee held her hands, swallowing down a knot of fear. "No, honey. I've known you since you were born."

Addison's frown deepened, her puzzlement increasing. "Were you and my mom friends?"

"I didn't know your mom, but I knew you." Renee pressed her lips together, struggling to find the next words.

Then, thankfully, Tate placed one hand on her shoulder, the other and Addison's.

"Renee is trying to tell you that she's your biological mother. She was the one who had you as a baby."

Addison looked from Tate to Renee, as if trying to absorb this.

"You had me as a baby?" she asked Renee.

All Renee could do was nod, fighting down her tears, swallowing her apprehension.

"And you gave me away?"

The confusion in her voice was almost her undoing but Renee knew she had to keep her focus on Addison. Not on her own struggle.

"I didn't give you away," Renee said, struggling to find a way to parse her own confused emotions. "I wanted you but I couldn't take care of you."

Addison could only stare at her and Renee felt hope for a relationship between her and Tate slipping away.

"You didn't want me."

"I did, honey, I did," Renee pleaded. "I wanted you so badly." She couldn't stop her voice breaking.

Addison looked confused and she turned to Tate, as if hoping he could enlighten her.

"Why was she mad at me? Why didn't she want me?"

Tate bit his lip and Renee could see he was struggling as much as she was.

He knelt down and turned her to face him. "Honey, remember Talia? Remember how she didn't work with you on your Math Facts and you were mad at her?"

Addison frowned and nodded.

"Do you remember why she didn't work with you?"

"Yes. Because she had to help Natasha."

"And she had to help Natasha because Talia knew you were really good at Math Facts but Natasha wasn't. Natasha needed some extra help. And you didn't."

"Yes. I remember."

"Renee, your mother, had the same thing. Her mother was really sick and she was sad about that. You know her mother is in a wheelchair, right?"

Addison nodded.

"Well, Renee had to take care of her mother. And she couldn't take care of you too. But Renee knew that you were going into our family. Me and your mom. And that you would be okay. That you would be taken care of. But there was no one else to take care of her mother."

"I wanted to take care of you," Renee said, taking a chance and laying her hand on Addison's shoulder. "I wanted to have you so bad. I really did."

Addison looked at her, as if seeing her in a different light. Through a different lens.

"I like you," she said, seeming to be puzzled at the conundrum of being angry with her biological mother and yet liking this woman in front of her. "I like you a lot."

"And that's good. I'm so glad you do. Because I not only like you, I love you." Renee took a chance and squeezed her shoulder just a little more. "I love you so much."

Addison blinked and the tear that drifted down her cheek, gutted her.

"Oh, honey, please don't cry," Renee choked out and fighting down her self-imposed restraint, she pulled the little girl into her arms.

Addison fought for only a moment and then collapsed against her, clinging to her.

Renee felt Addison's hands cling to her, clinging to her heart, settling into her soul.

"Oh, honey, I love you so much."

Addison trembled in her arms and then, finally, drew away. She looked over at Tate then at Renee.

"We both love you," Tate said, stroking her hair. "And now we are all together."

Her daughter sniffed, then swiped at her eyes, looking at Renee. "But my mom is still my mom, right?"

"Of course, honey," Renee said. "Your mom will always be your mom. But I'm hoping that I can have a small piece of your heart too."

Addison seemed to consider that then nodded. "You can have a big piece," she said.

Renee almost wilted in relief, so thankful that they had navigated this tricky path.

Tate reached over and took her hand, then Addison's. Addison took Renee's to close the circle. She smiled, glancing from Tate to Renee. "I'm so lucky," she said. "I will get to have two moms."

Tate chuckled and pulled both Addison and Renee into his arms. They stayed that way a moment, then Addison wriggled free.

"And maybe we can make another scrapbook," she said.

"I think we could do that," Renee said, her heart full of gratitude and love.

"And Daddy can help again."

Tate groaned and Renee chuckled. "I think that's a great idea," she said.

"I thought you were on my side," Tate grumbled as they stood.

EPILOGUE

"Delicious. Simply delicious," Arlan said, wiping his mouth with a napkin and leaning away from a table still full of Parmesan-coated chicken breasts, stuffed potatoes, avocado-and-spinach salad and glazed baby carrots.

All made by Renee and her mother.

"I was going to say that," Tate protested, reaching beside him and squeezing Renee's hand. "If we eat like this every day, I'm going to have to go to the gym more often."

Renee's happiness bubbled over into a smile that had been a permanent feature for the past week.

Ever since she and Tate had walked down to the river. Ever since they had talked to Addison.

"I'm glad you could come," was all she said.

"Wouldn't have missed it." Then, without a hint of self-consciousness, Tate leaned over and kissed her.

"Can we have dessert now?" Addison said, fairly bouncing on her chair, her happiness as contagious as Renee's.

"Did you make it?" Renee asked with a grin.

Addison shook her head. "We bought it at the bakery, and it's a special, special cake for my special, special mom." She gave Renee a self-conscious smile. "That's you."

Renee's old pain deep within her faded away at the sound of those words on her daughter's lips.

"Let's go get it," Tate said, pushing himself away from the table.

Renee heard giggling, then a warning from Tate. The snick of something and then a sizzling.

What on earth?

The door of the bedroom creaked open, and then Addison appeared with a cake with a blazing sparkler in its middle.

She had a solemn look on her face as she walked toward the table, Tate behind her, guiding her.

"Is it your birthday?" Arlan asked, obviously as mystified as Renee was.

Renee shook her head as Addison set the cake on the table in front of her. Then Addison looked up at her father, who nodded.

Addison cleared her throat, then held her hand out to her father. Together they both dropped down on one knee, each holding their other hand out to Renee.

She took Addison's hand in one hand and Tate's in the other, completing the circle.

Then Tate and Addison said together, "Renee, will you marry us?"

Renee could only stare, as the five simple words registered in her brain.

Then her eyes tingled, and her happiness burst out in a flood of tears.

"Yes. Oh, yes," she choked out through the tears.

"I thought she would be happy," Addison whispered to Tate.

"She is," Tate whispered back.

Then Renee leaned forward and gathered them in a three-way hug.

"I love you. Love you so much," she said.

"We love you, too," Addison said, flinging her arms around Renee's neck. Renee closed her eyes, holding the little girl close.

Tate managed to drop a kiss on Renee's mouth.

Then he reached over and lifted the sparkler from the cake. At its base lay a gold ring with a sparkling diamond.

"It still has frosting on it," he grumbled with a frown, but Renee held out her hand, and he slipped it on, leaving a trail of white icing.

The diamond sparkled on her hand, and Renee felt tears threaten again.

"This calls for a toast and a blessing," Arlan said in a choked voice. He stood smiling down at the three of them, raising a glass with one hand, his other clinging to Brenda's, who was watching the scene, her own eyes shining with tears.

"May God bless you and keep you," he said. "May His light shine on you, and may you live your life as a family that serves and loves Him."

A family.

Renee looked over at Tate, then at her daughter, and leaned into Tate's embrace.

"We're a family," she whispered in awe.

"I love the sound of that," Tate replied. Then he kissed her again.

A family, together at last.

OTHER SERIES

I have many other books for you to enjoy. Check them out here.

FAMILY BONDS

#1 SEEKING HOME

A rancher who suffered a tragic loss. A single mother on the edge. Can these two find the courage to face a romantic new beginning?

#2 CHOOSING HOME

If you like emergency room drama, second chances, and quaint small-town settings, then you'll adore this romance.

#3 COMING HOME

He thought she chose a hotel over him. She thought he loved money more than her. Years later, can they fill the emptiness in their hearts?

#4 FINDING HOME

She's hiding a terrible truth. He's trying to overcome his scandalous history. Together, forgiveness might give them a second chance.

FAMILY TIES

Four siblings trying to finding their way back to family and faith

A COWBOY'S REUNION

He's still reeling from the breakup. She's ashamed of what she did. Can a chance reunion mend the fence, or are some hearts forever broken? If you like second chance stories, buried passions, and big country settings, then you'll love this emotional novel.

"I enjoyed this book and had trouble putting it down and had to finish it. If the rest of this series is this great, I look forward to reading more books by Carolyne Aarsen." Karen Semones - Amazon Review

THE COWBOY'S FAMILY

She's desperate. He's loyal. Will a dark lie hold them back from finding love on the ranch? If you like determined heroines, charming cowboys, and family dramas, then you'll love this heartfelt novel.

"What a wonderful series! The first book is Cowboy's Reunion. Tricia's story begins in that book. Emotional stories with wonderful characters. Looking forward to the rest of the books in this series." Jutzie - Amazon reviewer

TAMING THE COWBOY

A saddle bronc trying to prove himself worthy to a father who never loved him. A wedding planner whose ex-fiancee was too busy chasing his own dreams to think of hers. Two people, completely wrong for each other who yet need each other in ways they never realized. Can they let go of their own plans to find a way to heal together?

"This is the third book in the series and I have loved them all. . . . can't wait to see what happens with the last sibling." - Amazon reviewer

THE COWBOY'S RETURN

The final book in the Family Ties Series:

He enlisted in the military, leaving his one true love behind.

She gave herself to a lesser man and paid a terrible price.

In their hometown of Rockyview, they can choose to come together or say a final goodbye...

"This author did an amazing job of turning heartache into happiness with realism and inspirational feeling." Marlene - Amazon Reviewer

❧❦❧❦❧

SWEETHEARTS OF SWEET CREEK

Come back to faith and love

#1 HOMECOMING

Be swept away by this sweet romance of a woman's search for belonging and second chances and the rugged rancher who helps her heal.

#2 - HER HEARTS PROMISE

When the man she once loved reveals a hidden truth about the past, Nadine has to choose between justice and love.

#3 - CLOSE TO HIS HEART

Can love triumph over tragedy?

#4 - DIVIDED HEARTS

To embrace a second chance at love, they'll need to discover the truths of the past and the possibilities of the future…

#5 - A HERO AT HEART

If you like rekindled chemistry, family drama, and small, beautiful towns, then you'll love this story of heart and heroism.

#6 - A MOTHER'S HEART

If you like matchmaking daughters, heartfelt stories of mending broken homes, and fixer-upper romance, then this story of second chances is just right for you.

❦❦❦❦

HOLMES CROSSING SERIES

The Only Best Place is the first book in the Holmes Crossing Series.

#1 THE ONLY BEST PLACE

One mistake jeopardized their relationship. Will surrendering her dreams to save their marriage destroy her?

#2 ALL IN ONE PLACE

She has sass, spunk and a haunting secret.

#3 THIS PLACE

Her secret could destroy their second chance at love

#4 A SILENCE IN THE HEART

Can a little boy, an injured kitten and a concerned vet with his own past pain, break down the walls of Tracy's heart?

#5 ANY MAN OF MINE

Living with three brothers has made Danielle tired of guys and cowboys. She wants a man. But is she making the right choice?

#6 A PLACE IN HER HEART

Her new boss shattered her dreams and now she has to work with him. But his vision for the magazine she loves puts them at odds. Can they find a way to work together or will his past bitterness blind him to future love.

Made in the USA
Monee, IL
30 September 2021

79097685R00114